BLACKSTONE RANGER ROGUE

Blackstone Rangers Book 4

ALICIA MONTGOMERY

Also by Alicia Montgomery

THE TRUE MATES SERIES

Fated Mates

Blood Moon

Romancing the Alpha

Witch's Mate

Taming the Beast

Tempted by the Wolf

THE LONE WOLF DEFENDERS SERIES

Killian's Secret

Loving Quinn

All for Connor

THE TRUE MATES STANDALONE NOVELS

Holly Jolly Lycan Christmas

A Mate for Jackson: Bad Alpha Dads

TRUE MATES GENERATIONS

A Twist of Fate

Claiming the Alpha

Alpha Ascending

A Witch in Time

Highland Wolf

COPYRIGHT © 2020 ALICIA MONTGOMERY
WWW.ALICIAMONTGOMERYAUTHOR.COM
FIRST ELECTRONIC PUBLICATION OCTOBER 2020

EDITED BY LAVERNE CLARK
COVER BY JACQUELINE SWEET
102120

Chapter 1

Darcey Wednesday sighed as she watched the happy couple dance to the slow, romantic song playing over the speakers. The ballroom of The Blackstone Grand Hotel was decorated beautifully, setting up a fairy-tale-like background for the bride and groom.

Really, she was ecstatic for Daniel and Sarah. If anyone deserved to live happily ever after, it was her sister. Ever since they met at that god-awful foster home, Sarah had taken care of her and their other adopted sibling, Adam. For over twelve years, Sarah had been like their mother, father, protector, and caregiver all in one. She could have abandoned them when she turned eighteen and was no longer the responsibility of the state, but she didn't. Sarah worked her ass off to get them out of a terrible situation and provide for them all these years.

And now, Sarah had the love of her life, Daniel Rogers, to take care of her. And Darcey would never begrudge her sister happiness.

But that didn't mean she couldn't feel a pang of envy, watching them stare into each other's eyes, holding each other, dancing together. They were two bodies, but one soul. Fated, bonded mates.

Someone jostled her from behind, and she turned her head. It was one of the waiters carrying a tray of champagne as he walked away from her.

A fluttering in her chest distracted her for a moment.

Mine?

She shook her head and smiled sadly.

The fluttering slowed to a weak flapping before it stopped.

Another sigh escaped her lips. She was used to the familiar flutter and the voice in her head. After all, she was a shifter, and for as long as she could remember, had always shared her body with her inner animal. It never bothered her, that she was different. In fact, she wondered what it was like for humans like Sarah and Adam. What was it like to constantly be alone in their thoughts? To not have an inner companion? To not have to struggle to keep it under control?

Yes, most of her life, she'd lived around humans, from the Nevada orphanage where she'd spent the first nine years of her life, to the various foster homes she was shuttled around in until she met Sarah and Adam. Still, it wasn't something she thought about every day—that was just her life. Sure, she'd met a few shifters over the years. When she came close to any of them, she always just *knew* if they were like her. Like a feeling she couldn't describe but a truth she just knew.

Now, here she was, in Blackstone, Colorado, surrounded by other shifters. Hundreds of them. The moment she stepped foot in this town, she knew this place was way different from Las Vegas where she'd lived all her life. Soon, she would be living here full time, too, and opening the first ever brick and mortar shop of Silk, Lace, and Whispers, the online lingerie store she ran with Sarah.

It was exciting, for sure, and she was grateful that Daniel

had invited her to live with them in his house. She and Adam would be occupying two of the bedrooms on the first floor. She would be surrounded by her family—old and new, which included Daniel's parents who she was already growing to love —and would be living in a town where everyone was like *her*.

But she still felt alone. Like there was something out there she was constantly searching for. Like something was missing.

Maybe it was because she wasn't like other shifters here. Her new brother-in-law was a bear, as was his boss, Damon Cooper, whom she met earlier today. His other coworkers in the Blackstone Rangers were wolves, lions, deer, foxes, and of course, she had heard about the Blackstone dragons who protected the town.

But her? She was no apex predator. In fact, she wasn't any kind of predator. Rather, she was the most docile, harmless creature one could imagine—a swan.

She had only been a few days old when she appeared at the doorstep of the St. Margaret Orphanage. The nuns had no idea what she was and had been just as surprised as her when a few years later, she was in the middle of a fight with another kid and *poof*—disappeared under the pile of clothes on the floor. Panicked, she had dashed into the bathroom and saw her reflection in the full-length mirror. She looked like a fluffy gray duck. Yes, as cliched as it sounded—an ugly little duckling. But later on, as she matured, her true form emerged. The ugly duckling turned into a beautiful swan.

Kinda, anyway.

But surely there were other non-predatory shifters around here, right? A raccoon or squirrel, or maybe even other avian shifters?

The music shifted into something more cheerful, jarring her out of her thoughts. Daniel released Sarah and stepped back, then led her into the beginning steps of an old-fashioned swing dance. The crowd cheered and clapped as the couple spun around the dance floor.

"They're so happy, it's disgusting."

Darcey suppressed a smile at the familiar voice. "Disgusting, huh?" she said to her younger brother, Adam, who had popped up beside her in his brand-new motorized wheelchair.

"Yeah." His mouth twisted. "I don't see the big deal with being in love anyway. People can be happy on their own, you know?"

At first, she thought her brother was being his usual sarcastic teen self. But when he looked up at her with those big green eyes, she saw a flash of something that made her heart twitch. It was sympathy.

Aside from the couple themselves, no one was happier about Daniel and Sarah getting together than Adam was. He practically worshiped his new big brother and was thrilled about leaving Nevada to live here. But Adam was not only smart for his sixteen years, but also emotionally mature. She knew he was trying to suppress his happiness because of *her*. He didn't want her to feel bad that Sarah had Daniel, while Darcey remained single.

As far as she knew, Sarah had never dated seriously nor had any long-term boyfriends. In fact, except for two or three guys she'd dated exclusively for a few months and handful of dates over the years, Sarah had been contentedly single, devoting all her time to raising and providing for her and Adam.

She, on the other hand, tended to flit from one relationship to another, with disastrous results. Whenever a guy paid even a modicum of attention on her, she went all in, focusing her time and energy to making the "relationship" work, bending over backward to please him. But none of that mattered because they all ended the same—with her alone and her heart broken.

She was like a big jerk magnet, attracting only the worst men. They seemed nice enough at first, but they more often than not turned into assholes who either ghosted her or stuck around long enough to take advantage of her, whether financially or emotionally. Eventually, she would end up crying and swearing off relationships. But sure enough, a new guy would come along, and well ... her relationship status had more cycles than the Tour de France.

Her swan shook its head sadly.

Mine?

Sure, she could blame it all on her animal side. Weren't swans known for their fidelity, their propensity to mate for life? It seemed like it asked that question—*mine?*—whenever she met a new guy or was near any potential boyfriend. And Darcey was sure each one was "the one," and when it turned out he wasn't, her swan would peck and nag at her to keep looking.

But still, she couldn't help herself. She just wanted to be loved. Was that so bad?

"Sure, people can be content on their own," she said, repeating Adam's words, then placed a hand on his shoulder. "But we can also be happy for them without feeling like we're less for not having what they have." She gave his shoulder a squeeze, then smiled down at him. He smirked back at her in that way only teenagers can, and she chuckled.

Back on the dance floor, the music faded out, and Daniel dipped Sarah low and kissed her, much to the delight of the spectators.

"C'mon," she said. "I haven't talked to them the whole night. Let's go say hi." She hurried past all the other guests, who made way for them as they made a beeline for the couple. "Daniel, Sarah! That was a great dance set. I didn't even know you were going to do that."

Daniel flashed her a smile that reached all the way to his

bright silvery blue eyes. Leaning down, he kissed her on the cheek. "Hey, Darce. Are you having fun?"

That feeling came over her as she sensed his bear. She wasn't frightened or anything. In fact, his animal's presence felt familial and protective. "Everyone's been great and ... it's weird being around so many people like me." He didn't ask about how she felt being surrounded by other shifters, but she could just tell it was on his mind.

"That's great, Darce, and how's the move?"

When he had asked her to come live with them in Blackstone, the choice was easy. She wasn't really attached to Las Vegas, plus, with their online sales skyrocketing, she and Sarah realized they could open their shop here instead of their original plan of starting it in Summerlin, not to mention, quit her old crappy retail job. The day she'd handed in her notice to her awful boss Agnes was one of the happiest in her life. "One more trip back to Vegas in the morning and I'm done." All she had to do was pick up the last of their stuff at their old apartment, hand in the keys to the landlord, and drive back.

"Thank God," Adam groaned. "I'm so glad to be out of that town."

"Looking forward to the fall?" Daniel asked. Adam was set to start school at the local high school, one that Daniel himself had attended.

"Yeah, yeah," the teen said. "Ugh, can I go back up to the suite now? This party's so boring and everyone's so old."

Sarah chuckled. "All right. Go on ahead."

"Later," he said as he drove away.

"Go straight to the room!" Sarah called out. "And don't even think about going through the mini bar!" But Adam only answered with a dismissive wave.

Daniel turned to her. "Do you want to dance, Darcey?"

It was really sweet of him to ask, and she was about to say yes when the fluttering in her chest came back.

Mine?

"Um, maybe later?" She wrinkled her nose. A strange tingling came over her as her swan beat its wings madly.

Mine?

"I think ... I think I need to go somewhere ..."

Her feet took her away from the dance floor like they had a life of their own. The flapping of wings inside her was so loud, the noise and music around her faded away. Her swan frantically swung its head side to side as if searching for something. Feeling her swan's frenetic energy, she had no choice but be swept away by its whim, and she dashed across the ballroom, sidestepping other guests.

Mine?

Her vision tunneled, focusing on a pinpoint, leading her toward the bar. There were several people there, but one particular person caught her attention despite the fact that his back was to her and she could only make out dark hair and broad shoulders. Her hand reached out and tapped him on the arm. "Excuse me," she breathed out.

Slowly, he turned around. His dark head was bowed, his gaze going immediately to the exposed cleavage of her low-cut dress. "Hey, sweetheart." A smile spread across his lips as his head slowly tilted up. "What can I do for—"

Mine!

"—you?"

Light golden-brown eyes stared right into her, sending electricity across her skin as she heard something from deep within him answer back: *Mine.*

"Yes," she gasped. "It's me." Her swan squawked animatedly. This was it. It was *him.*

When she heard that Sarah and Daniel were mates, she

almost didn't believe it. Growing up, with no one to explain to her what being a shifter was all about, she could only do her own research on the Internet, and even then, the information was not really accurate or scientific.

But she had heard about mates—that fate paired shifters with someone they were intended to be with and that only those with animals inside them would be able to tell who their mate was.

She mentally slapped her forehead. God, she was so dumb. Her swan was looking, looking, looking all the time. Trying to find him in all those guys she dated. Asking that question —*mine?*—and never getting an answer back because they were all wrong.

But now, he was here. Even though she didn't realize that she was looking for him, she knew it: He was the one she had been searching for.

And, oh dear, he was *breathtaking*. He was tall, a couple of inches over six feet with a lean, graceful build. He wasn't overly hulking like Daniel or many of the shifters here, but his shoulders were broad, and his biceps strained against his shirt. He was handsome, too, with firm lips and a chiseled, clean-shaven jaw, but what she couldn't tear her gaze away from was his eyes. They were the color of molten honey, and she wanted to lose herself in them.

Joy burst through her, making her heart leap out of her chest. She couldn't stop the smile on her face, even if she'd wanted to. Looking up at him, she could see the shock register on his face as his eyes widened and his jaw slackened.

"Yo, Anders!" someone called from behind. "You joining us?"

He didn't answer, just kept staring at her. Darcey couldn't move either. His companion peeked from behind him, said something, then shrugged and walked away.

Time ticked by, with neither of them saying anything or moving. Finally, she managed a breath and lunged forward, wrapping her arms around him. *Oh God, he smelled so good.* "I can't believe it," she whispered. "I didn't think I'd find you."

He tensed in her arms, and something in her brain got through the blissful cloud surrounding her. Frowning, she released him and stepped back. "Your name is Anders? I'm Darcey. Darcey Wednesday. I'm your—"

"I know who you are."

Of course he did. This actually made it easier. Sarah had told her that although Daniel had known instantly she was his mate, she didn't know because she was human, and that had caused some problems between them initially. "Great. So ... do you want to, like, go somewhere to talk? Or you can meet my family?"

His nostrils flared, and his jaw hardened. "No, I don't think so."

Oh God, she sounded stupid. Maybe they were supposed to do something else? "Oh. Okay. What do you want to do, then?"

His Adam's apple bobbed as he swallowed hard. "Listen, Daisy—"

"Darcey," she corrected. Her swan pecked its beak toward him irritably.

"Yeah. Okay. I don't do relationships."

She blinked. "Excuse me?"

The corner of his mouth quirked up. "You seem like a sweet girl, Darla. But I'm not the one for you."

Was he joking? "B-but I heard it. My animal said it. And yours—"

"Be that as it may, this just isn't going to work out, Dolly."

"But we're—"

"I like what I see, though." His voice dipped low, and he lifted his hand, tracing a finger over her arm, up to her shoulder and collarbone, then followed the vee of her dress down her chest.

Warmth spread through her as she closed her eyes, and she bit her lip to keep from moaning when his knuckles brushed the tops of her breasts.

"You're pretty enough, and I'm not picky. Wanna go meet me in the janitor's closet for a quick screw? This party's getting boring anyway."

His words slammed into her, making her eyes snap open. "A-a quick screw? That's what you want?"

"Yeah, sure." He pulled his hand away. "But it won't mean anything. If you're looking for someone to take you on romantic dates and whisper sweet nothings and live happily ever after with, then go find someone else. I prefer my lays with no strings attached."

This wasn't happening. Surely this was some kind of joke. "I ... I don't believe you. You don't mean what you're saying." He must have felt it too. She *heard* his animal roar it out. What was he anyway?

A vision flashed in her head. Something big with large teeth and sharp claws. Stripes and fur and—

He let out a sardonic laugh. "I meant every word, sweetheart." The endearment dripped with acid. "If you don't want to get hurt, stay away from me." Turning on his heel, he put the glass in his hand back on the bar and walked away.

She stood there, frozen. Afraid to make a sound. Afraid to make a move. She was still as a statue, calm as a millpond on the outside.

But inside, a storm of emotions churned. Her swan cried out in distress, not knowing what was happening. The only thing it could focus on was that he—their mate—was walking away from them.

Her chest began to ache something fierce. It started small at first, like a tiny hairline crack along the edges of an icy river. But then it began to expand and grow until it felt like something inside her split apart. Tears sprung in her eyes and the only thing she knew right now was that she *had to get out of there.* Before she had a full-on break down.

Somehow, she managed to pry her feet from where they were stuck to the ground and began to walk. One foot in front of the other. No one was paying any mind to her as they laughed and danced and drank like there was nothing wrong in the world. She nearly made it out when she halted right by the exit. Her swan begged her to go back. To find their mate and make him see. Make him listen.

"He doesn't want us," she whispered.

"Darce?" It was Sarah. Her sister's hand landed on her shoulder and spun her around. "What's the—" Sarah sucked in a breath. "Are you crying?"

Her hands automatically brushed the tears spilling down her cheeks. "Nothing," she cried. "It's nothing."

"It's obviously *not* nothing." Sarah's brown eyes blazed as she gripped both her arms. "What's the matter? Tell me why you're crying."

"Did someone hurt you?" Daniel said in a menacing tone. "Tell me."

The outrage from Daniel's inner bear made her jump. She didn't even realize he was right there too. Because of course he was. He would be beside Sarah for the rest of their lives. He would never leave her or tell her to stay away.

"No. Not intentionally," she whispered. How could she even begin to explain it? "At least I don't think so ... I'm sorry, I have to go. I'm gonna go to my room. I just need to be alone for a bit." Shrugging off Sarah's grasp, she turned and sprang toward the elevators. Frantically, she tapped on the call button, waiting for the doors to open and darted inside as soon as the car arrived. However, as the doors were about to close, she saw Sarah running toward her.

"Stop!" Her sister made it just in time to slip her fingers between the doors. Stepping inside, she took Darcey by the shoulders. "Tell me what's wrong."

She shook her head. Her throat burned so bad that she was scared to speak.

"Darce." Sarah's tone was firmer now. "You know I'm going to hound you until you tell me what's wrong. I'm going to stay here and miss my entire reception if I have to, but I won't leave until I find out who hurt you and make them pay. Please."

Slowly, she lifted her head and stared up at her sister's face. They weren't biological sisters, not even close. But they were sisters of the heart, bound together by the vow they made the day they met at that miserable foster home. It was the first time she ever felt real love, and maybe the last.

"Oh, Sarah," she cried, then burst into tears.

"Darce. Oh no." Sarah's arms wound around her. "C'mon, let's go to your room."

Thank goodness Sarah was there, because otherwise, Darcey wouldn't have known how to get back to her room. Once they were inside, her sister sat her down on the bed, got a cold, wet towel from the bathroom and pressed it to her face, all the while soothing her as she cried.

When the tears finally slowed down, Sarah took her hand in hers. "Now tell me what happened."

Sarah always made her feel safe, so Darcey told her everything. Every single, humiliating detail of that short conversation with her mate. It was obvious her sister was outraged, and Darcey would always be grateful for the fact that she had her back all this time.

"Who was it?" Sarah asked.

"I don't know ... never met him before. Though someone called him Anders."

Sarah's face completely changed from sympathetic to pure, deep anger. "A-Anders? Anders Stevens is your *mate*?"

She sniffed. "I didn't get his last name. But how many Anders could there be?"

Her sister shot to her feet, hands fisting at her sides. "For his sake, it better be another Anders who made you cry." She bared her teeth. "I don't care if he's Daniel's friend or that he can turn into a tiger, I'm going to kill that motherfucker!"

"Sarah, no!" Her inner swan protested too. "I mean ... please don't make a big deal—"

"Not a big deal?" she said incredulously. "Saying all those things to you ... even if he wasn't your mate, I would still kick his ass."

"Sarah ..." Grabbing her arm, she dragged her sister back down next to her. "Please ... I just want to forget this night ever happened."

"Oh, sweetie ..." Sarah put an arm around her and pulled her close. "It'll be all right. You'll be all right."

Would she? But instead of saying that, she nodded. "You're right. Just ... just don't tell anyone, okay?"

Sarah hesitated. "I won't tell just anyone. But Daniel ... I can't keep this from him."

"I ..." She bit her lip. Sarah was right, of course. Daniel was her mate. If she kept things from him, he would probably be hurt. "All right, but he won't tell anyone else, right? Not even Adam?"

"No, he won't, I promise."

She let out a relieved sigh, though the tightness in her chest did not go away. "Thank you, Sarah. For being here."

"Of course. I love you, Darce. I'll be here for you anytime."

Slumping over, she buried her face in Sarah's shoulder. "Love you, too, Sarah."

———

Darcey was glad she had to go back to Las Vegas the next day. The long drive would be a good distraction. Of course, Sarah insisted on coming along with her. Though she protested because it was a day after the reception, her sister insisted and said Daniel was okay with it. She didn't ask her what her husband's reaction was to what happened last night, but knowing how protective Daniel was, he probably wasn't happy about it. But Sarah assured her that Daniel wouldn't say anything to anyone.

The trip to Vegas and back was uneventful, and Sarah did her best to cheer her up during their road trip. Truthfully, it did work. At least for the human part of her. Her brain was telling her that she had only met the guy for five seconds, and moping after a rejection that fast was pathetic, even for her.

But her swan ... it was inconsolable. It pined and cried and hung its long graceful neck low, like it was legitimately sick. Maybe it was, because there were times when Darcey herself wanted to throw up. Other times, she was just genuinely sick of feeling sick. But she didn't know what to do.

Now, here she was, a week later, in her bed alone on a Saturday morning, and the moment she opened her eyes, all she wanted to do was go back to blissful sleep.

"Get up!"

"What? I—hey!" The covers flew off her. "I—Sarah?"

Her sister stood at the foot of her bed, hands on her hips. "You're done with this shit."

She sat up. "I am?"

Sarah nodded. "It's been a week since the reception. You can't sit around moping all day—"

"I am not moping," she protested. "Besides, I've been to the shop with you every day, getting the store ready, doing inventory—"

"You're there, physically," Sarah said. "But you're not *there*, there. I'm not blind, Darce." With a deep sigh, she sat down on the mattress. "You're in pain. I can feel it."

"Just leave me alone, Sarah," she said, plopping back on the pillows. "I'll get through this, I always do." Her swan let out a pathetic *meep* and shook its wings.

"I know you will. But I'm not going to leave you alone." Grabbing her arm, she hauled Darcey out of bed. "Get dressed, we're leaving."

"Leaving?" she sputtered as Sarah dragged her to the bathroom. "Where are we going?"

"Out," she said. "First, we're going to a yoga class, and then we're going to do some retail therapy, and then lunch."

"But I don't—" It was too late. Sarah had pushed her into the bathroom and slammed the door shut.

"The only way I'm opening this door," her sister shouted through the door, "Is if you're washed up and ready to go."

And so that's how Darcey found herself at the Blackstone Bodyworx eight o'clock yoga class. The studio was located in the same complex as the Silk, Lace, and Whisper's soon-to-open boutique. She had met the owner, Anna Victoria, a couple times including during the reception as she was also Damon Cooper's mate.

"Just breathe. Listen to your body. Listen to yourself," Anna Victoria instructed as she led the class through the final poses. "You may not be able to control what goes on outside, but you can control what goes on inside."

Darcey focused on Anna Victoria's words as she twisted her

body into position. *Maybe this was a good idea.* Sarah, who was on the mat next to her, looked over at her and flashed her a smile, which she returned. Yoga was her sister's thing, though she had joined her a couple of times, but it never really stuck. However, today, it helped her feel calmer.

"You're all wonderful, strong, beautiful people," Anna Victoria said as they began to ease down on the mat. "Close your eyes and tell that to yourself. If you need it now, especially, tell yourself that you're strong, independent, and worthy of being alive. Worthy of existing, with all the wonderful imperfections that make up who you are."

It was at that moment that something broke inside of Darcey, because she found herself bursting into tears. Sarah immediately sat up, as did several of the other students, who stared at her.

Humiliated, Darcey shot up and dashed toward the locker room, heading into a stall and shutting it behind her. *Well,* she thought glumly as she sobbed. *At least I made it almost a week without crying.* And truly, it was amazing that the last time she'd cried was that night at the reception.

"Darce?" came the hesitant voice of her sister from the other side of the door.

"Give me a minute, Sarah," she sniffed. Unrolling some tissue, she wiped her face, dabbed at her eyes, and blew her nose before pushing the stall door open. "I—oh." Warmth crept up her neck as she realized Sarah wasn't alone. Two other girls were behind her, including Anna Victoria. "Sorry," she said to the instructor. "It's not you, it's me."

Anna Victoria smiled at her weakly. "No, don't worry about it. Usually, I make girls cry in the middle of class, not at the end."

"You okay, hon?" The other girl asked, her face a mask of concern. Unlike most of the girls in class who were geared up in fancy yoga attire and makeup, she was bare-faced and dressed in an old T-shirt and shorts, while her messy blonde hair was pulled back in a haphazard ponytail. If Darcey remembered correctly, this was J.D.

"I'm ... all right now." Darcey swallowed, then made her way past the three women to sit down on the bench.

"Goddammit, I'm really going to kill him," Sarah whispered as she sat down next to Darcey.

"Kill who?" J.D. asked.

"You heard that?" Sarah asked.

"She's a shifter," Darcey said with a sniff. She knew it right away. J.D. had the scent of fur and something ... vicious.

"So," J.D. plopped down on Darcey's other side and steepled her fingers together. "Who are we going to kill?"

Sarah looked at her helplessly.

Darcey shrugged. "My mate," she sighed.

"Your mate?" Anna Victoria asked. "You have a mate? You never said anything about having a mate before."

"I just met him," she said. "At the reception last week."

"And the damn asshole rejected her," Sarah muttered through gritted teeth.

"What?" J.D. snarled. "Who the fuck is this guy who would reject a hottie with a sweet ass like Darcey?"

When Sarah caught her gaze, she nodded. "Who else?" her sister spat. "Anders Stevens."

"That motherfucker!" J.D. shot to her feet. "We are going to make his striped ass suffer."

"Please, don't," Darcey said. "I just ... I just want to forget about him."

"Don't worry, it'll work out," Anna Victoria said. "I mean, Damon didn't want to bond with me at first, but we got together. Shifters can't ignore their inner instinct."

"Sounds like they can," Darcey said sadly. "It was just ... like a switch for him." And so once again, she repeated the events of that night to them.

"*Pshaw*," J.D. said dismissively. "You don't want him anyway. Anders is a grade A, man-whoring asshole."

Darcey winced. The thought of Anders with another woman did not sit well with her swan. It flapped its wings in distress and let out a sad, protesting *honk*.

"J.D.!" Sarah warned. "She doesn't need to hear that part about him."

"Well, it's his own damned fault, with his reputation," J.D. said. "But seriously, hon, you dodged a big bullet. You should be thanking your lucky stars that he saved you the trouble of getting hurt in the first place."

"I should?" Because it sure didn't feel like she was lucky.

"Yeah," J.D. insisted. "But you can't mope around like a sad, heartbroken little bird."

Did J.D. know what she was? Of course she did. Just like she could tell J.D. was ... something feline. "I don't know what I'm supposed to do."

"Remember what I said in class?" Anna Victoria said. "You're a strong, independent woman. You'll be fine. You're going to get through this."

"And we're going to help," J.D. said, a smile forming on her face.

Anna Victoria's brows snapped together. "We are?"

"Yes!" J.D. paced back and forth.

"I can see the wheels turning in her head," Sarah stage-whispered to Anna Victoria.

"What are you planning, J.D.?" Anna Victoria asked.

"Darcey," J.D. began, ignoring the other two and kneeling down in front of her. "You're beautiful, kind, sexy, and more important—stronger than you think."

"I-I am?"

"Yeah," Sarah piped in.

"You're the strong one, Sarah." Darcey sniffed. "You're the one who got us out of that awful foster home."

"I'm not talking about that." Her sister smiled. "How many times have you laid your heart on the line, only to have some guy stomp all over it? How many times have you cried over a man, yet brushed yourself off and got back on your feet? You've loved and lost and loved and lost again. You can do this."

"I—" Something in her sister's words struck a chord deep in her. "You're right." A breath escaped her throat. It was a revelation of some sort. Like choirs of angels coming down from heaven, except, instead of singing about true love, they were singing a different message. Sure, right now it sounded like they were singing, *You've been acting like an idiot, Darcey!* in four-part harmony, but it was exactly what she needed to hear. "You're so right, Sarah!"

"I am?" Sarah blinked.

"Yeah." Brushing off some imaginary dust off her thighs, she got up. "I don't need a mate to make me happy. In fact, maybe I don't need any mate at all."

"Huh?" Sarah looked flummoxed. "Er, that's true but that's not exactly what I—"

"You said it, sister!" J.D. raised a hand.

She slapped her palm to J.D.'s. "Relationships just mess you up and stop you from achieving your goals." And she already knew what she wanted to be. Just like Anna Victoria said. Strong. Independent. A new Darcey.

"Sure, but ..." Anna Victoria looked around nervously. "I mean, when you meet the right guy, it won't be like that."

J.D. wiggled her eyebrows suggestively. "Blackstone has a ton of hot guys. I mean, have you *seen* our fire department? If it wasn't illegal, I'd be setting fires every day to make them come to my house." She fanned herself suggestively.

"Oooh." Darcey clapped her hands together. "I'm down for some firemen."

"I thought men messed you up, Darce?" Sarah said.

"I said *relationships* messed me up," Darcey shot back. "What I need is to break out of my bad habit of going all in with *one* man. To stop serving up my own heart on a platter." That particular organ would stay locked up in her damned chest for once. "And I need to stop being so desperate."

"Darce, you are *not* desperate," Sarah protested.

"What about that time I drove four hours so I could 'accidentally' bump into that lawyer I was so sure was 'the one'?" Darcey cringed at the memory. She and that guy had only been on one date when he mentioned that he was going to a resort in Palm Springs that weekend for a wedding. After finding out where it was, she drove there, dressed to the nines, hoping to bump into him. She did eventually. In the elevator, heading back to his room with a bridesmaid.

"But you didn't give up."

"Yeah," she said wryly. "After that, I met that guy who played in that terrible cover band. I went to every single one of their gigs and pretended to like their music. He went on tour, and I never saw him again."

Sarah huffed. "If he couldn't see how special you were, then that was his problem, not yours."

"Or what about that guy whose parents I wanted to meet after three dates? Or that one who freaked out after I showed up at his job unannounced to surprise him with flowers?"

"Darce—"

"It's a cycle, see? I'm always the one going over the top and sacrificing everything for these guys. And I can't be that person anymore. I don't *want* to be that person." When Sarah looked at her skeptically, she put her hands up. "Look, I'm not turning into a man-hater. I'm just going to take it easy and keep my options open." And stop acting like a damned fool for once.

"That's the spirit," J.D. said. "Now, we should do some planning. I have other ideas too. How about we head over to The Den—"

"It's nine o'clock in the morning," Anna Victoria reminded her.

"I meant, tonight," J.D. said, then she grimaced. "You're right, though, forget The Den. Too many losers hang out there."

From the way she said losers, Darcey could guess exactly who she meant. "Should we go somewhere else?"

J.D. thought for a moment. "How about a girls' night at my place?"

"I'm in," Darcey said. Oh, she hadn't had a girls' night in, well, ever. Sarah was really the only woman she hung out and got along with. God, had she really spent most of her adult life chasing after men? Well, maybe it was time they chased after *her*.

"C'mon now, don't be spoilsports," J.D. said to Anna Victoria and Sarah. "I bet I could convince Temperance to join us and bring some of her pies."

"Fine," Anna Victoria relented. "I'll call Damon."

"See?" J.D. put an arm around Darcey. "*We* don't have to call anyone." She stuck her tongue out playfully at Anna Victoria, who only laughed. "Now, I have a couple of ideas. Not just to help your quest to break your bad habits, but also, to help your business. And have some fun along the way."

Now Darcey was *really* intrigued. "Really? What?"

"I'll tell you," J.D. said with a twinkle in her eyes. "But this is a conversation that needs alcohol. Lots of it, if you and I are going to get even a slight buzz."

Chapter 2

Anders Stevens knew that hanging out at The Den on a Sunday night was pathetic, even for him, but he couldn't help himself. Being out here meant that he didn't have to stay at home alone. Surrounded by the same four walls of his trailer. Surrounded by the silence or the hum of the sports channel on TV which couldn't drown out his loudest thoughts. Or the angriest growls of his tiger.

Even now, it raked its claws down his insides and let out a furious roar.

Cut that shit out!

Years of training and discipline had allowed him complete mastery of his tiger. While most shifters could live in harmony with their animals or bid them what to do, Anders could practically grab his tiger by the scruff and tell it to *pipe down*. And it worked too.

Usually.

The tiger craned its neck away from him. It let out an annoyed chuff and went to the corner and sulked.

His fingers flexed around the cool glass in his hand. He'd been so desperate to quiet down his animal that he'd actually ordered a shot of gin on the rocks. But he'd been staring at it for what seemed like hours until the ice melted, watering down the alcohol.

Yet he hadn't taken a sip or even a sniff. He hadn't had alcohol in years, and this was the closest he'd been to being tempted. After three weeks of fighting with himself and with his tiger, he was willing to give his soul to the Devil himself if it would fill in the big gaping hole in his chest.

Fuck.

He shut his eyes tight, but that made it worse. A vision of blue eyes—no, green—he shook his head. No, it was somewhere in between. Not quite green, not quite blue. Aquamarine maybe? He tried to Google it the other day, and that was the closest approximation he could find. Well, whatever the hell color those eyes were, the only thing he could remember was how they filled up with tears before he walked away from her.

Twenty-two days. Three hours. Twenty-six minutes. That was the first and last time he'd seen her. But she was in his thoughts nearly every moment of those twenty-two days, three hours, and twenty-six minutes, yet, he couldn't even say her damned name. Couldn't say what she was to him. No, he couldn't think of her or her eyes or her pink lips or that curvy body. Not when he heard that one word that announced his doom.

Mine.

He couldn't dare let his thoughts continue. Couldn't let his mind think about who she was and where she could be right now. It was so tempting to try and find out. Was she a friend of Daniel's? Or Sarah's? She couldn't have been from Blackstone. He'd lived here all his life and yet never met her. Surely someone as rare as an avian shifter would be well-known in town. Also, what kind of avian shifter was she? Owl? Hawk?

No, definitely not a predator bird. Something sweet and docile flashed in his mind.

His eyes flew open. *I need a distraction.* As a tiger shifter, his hearing was his best sense. Even in human form, he could focus it, as if he was actually in his animal form and rotate his ears like a radar dish, picking up bits of conversation here and there.

"I can't believe she left me for that—"

"Man, my boss is such a prick—"

"When didja get back, Nathan? How's Violet and the little one?"

"C'mon, she's so drunk, bet she won't even remember a thing from tonight."

That last one sent his senses tingling as his grip tightened on the glass. He turned his head slightly, trying to find out who was talking. It was the table of three men, two over from where he sat.

"... look at her, what a slut," one of them said.

"Bet she's a lot of fun," another added.

"And those tits," the last man said. "I'd like to get my hands on those."

"Well, I saw her first," the first one said. "Lemme finish this round, and I'm gonna go say hi."

Tamping down his rage, Anders slowly got up, trying not to attract attention. While most people thought he was loud and flashy, he could be stealthy if he wanted to be.

Scanning the room, it wasn't really hard to find out who those bastards were talking about. There was only one woman alone at the bar, a glass of wine sloshing in one hand while the other tried to catch Tim the bartender's attention.

"... can I have another, please, mister?" the brunette woman slurred as she waved her hand at Tim.

"Hey, sweetheart," Anders said, smoothly sidling up to the

woman. She swung her head up to look at him. Christ, she was no woman. She was practically a girl, though at least twenty-one if Tim served her alcohol. Did females grow younger each year? Or maybe he was just turning into an old man.

"Oh. Hey." A lazy smile spread across her face. "Where'd you come from?"

"From your dreams. Maybe tonight I can be in them again. Or in your bed." His mouth turned to dust at the thought, and his tiger roared in anger.

"*Oohhhh.*" She let out a giggle and reached over to squeeze his bicep. "Oh. My. God. You're, like, so built. You must work out."

"Some," he said. "But I get plenty of workout ... everywhere." He wiggled his eyebrows at her.

"Hmmm ..." Her face went all dreamy. "How about you buy me a drink, and we can talk more about working out."

"Sure, sweetheart." He caught the bartender's eye and cocked his head. "Hey, Tim, can you give my girl here—"

"Carrie," she supplied.

"Give my girl, Carrie, here my *favorite* drink. Extra strong."

Tim raised a bushy white brow but said nothing and turned around to start mixing the drink.

Thank you, Tim, he thought silently. Without the bartender's cooperation—or silence— over the years, everyone would have figured out by now that his favorite 'drink' was nothing more than soda water, a splash of cola syrup, and a squeeze of lime. It would surely ruin the reputation he'd been cultivating all these years if anyone suspected. But Carrie was three sheets to the wind, so she probably wouldn't notice.

"So, Carrie, tell me about yourself."

"Well," she began as she finished off her wine, "I'm a student at...."

He pasted a smile on his face and nodded, but glanced

behind him. That guy at the table who was planning on swooping in looked pissed off and stared daggers at him. *Good.* That should keep the asshole away.

But his job wasn't done yet. After two more orders of his favorite "drink" Anders put a couple of bills on the table. "How about we get out of here, Carrie?" he whispered in her ear.

Her fingers trailed up his chest. "I thought you'd never ask."

He placed a hand lightly on her lower back, and led her out of the bar. However, he must have underestimated how drunk she was because she stumbled forward, letting out a loud yelp. With an annoyed grunt, he caught her and hauled her up. "C'mon now."

"Are we going to your place?" she said in a way that was probably supposed to be sexy, but made him want to gag, especially when he got a whiff of alcohol from her breath.

"Sure, sweetheart, whatever you want. Did you drive here?"

"Keys in my purse. Blue Honda with the cat bumper stickers."

It took all his strength not to roll his eyes. "You won't be driving tonight, sweetheart, but I'll take care of it, okay? I'll take care of you."

"'Kay." Her eyes rolled back as he lifted her into his arms and walked her over to his pickup truck. Unlocking the front passenger door, he slid her into the seat. However, instead of closing the door, he reached over to the middle console and pulled out the water bottle he kept there and unscrewed the top.

Her head flopped forward, and she blinked.

"C'mon, sweetheart," he said, pushing the bottle to her mouth. "Have a sip. Do it for me, okay? I promise you'll feel better."

She grasped the bottle, put her mouth to it, then tipped it back.

"That's it ... slowly, slowly, you don't want to choke."

"I don't think you've got anything she's gonna choke on," came a voice from behind.

Anders tensed, then put the bottle down to her lap. "Hold onto this while I take care of something."

"Wh-what's going on?" she asked, before her head lolled back, passing out in half a second.

Slowly, Anders turned around. To his surprise, all three guys he heard talking about Carrie were there. "Can I help you, *gentlemen?*" He nearly choked on that last word.

The guy who was murdering Anders with his eyes earlier spoke up first. "Think you're so slick, swooping in and stealing that girl away from me?"

Oh, brother. Anders rolled his eyes. Not only did this guy sound like a prick, he looked like one, too, with his perfectly-styled blond hair, chino pants, and polo shirt. He even had a fucking sweater over his shoulders. "Did you get lost or something, son?" he began. "The nearest country club is about thirty miles that way. Don't forget to have your polo ponies scrubbed before you take them out for a ride."

His two friends, who were similarly dressed, chuckled.

Blondie sneered. "You piece of trash nobody."

Yeah, well better than being a piece of trash somebody who takes advantage of drunk women. But even though his tiger was raring for a fight, Anders kept his cool. "Whatever. As you can see, I'm busy here. Unlike you, I have places to be, women to do."

Obviously, Blondie didn't like that, and he stepped forward, hands raising. "Why you—"

"Doesn't seem like a fair fight, three against two."

Who the hell?

A shadowy figure stepped out from behind the Jeep parked across from him. Holy shit. *I must be hallucinating.*

But no, he wasn't. That was definitely John Krieger slowly

lumbering toward them. At nearly seven feet tall with broad hulking shoulders and tattoos down his massive arms, it was hard to mistake the former Master Sergeant turned ranger for anyone else. As he drew closer, Anders could feel the other man's animal—a grizzly bear, if he remembered correctly. The beast was like a tightly coiled spring ready to pounce. He'd gone into training with Krieger when he first signed up for the rangers five years ago, and he was man enough to admit that monster bear of his had made him wary. His tiger's instincts told him something was definitely wrong with this animal.

"Hey, hey," one of the other guys said with a nervous laugh. "Who said anything about a fight?"

"Yeah." The third guy put a hand on Blondie's shoulder. "C'mon, Bradley, time we go home. We have class tomorrow."

"Yeah, Bradley," Anders sneered. God, even his name made him sound like a cunt. "Go home."

Bradley looked from Krieger to Anders, then let out a huff. "Whatever. She's not worth it."

Anders watched as the three men—no, they were boys, really—walked away. Once they were out of sight, his shoulders relaxed. "You're a little far from home, aren't you, Krieger?"

After they'd finished training, the other man had been given a permanent assignment guarding the entrance up at Contessa Peak, in the highest and most remote area of the Blackstone Mountains. As far as he knew, Krieger never ventured far from his station as he hated being around others.

Krieger grunted. "Thought I'd come down for a cold beer."

"Right. Well, I should get going." He jerked his thumb back at Carrie, who was now snoring loudly from the front passenger seat. "Heard it was rude to keep a lady waiting." He pivoted on his heel and was about to shut the door when Krieger's words stopped him.

"Third time this month for you."

He ground his teeth. "We can't all live like monks, Krieg."

"I mean, third time you've brought a girl home—to her home—safely and kept assholes like Bradley from taking advantage of them."

He spun around. "How the hell did you know—are you following me? Sorry, dude, I don't swing that way."

Krieger snorted. "You can hide all you want, Stevens. I know what you really are."

"You do, huh, champ?" he mocked. "Mind your own business, and shut your trap." *Fuck.* Having Krieger sniff around was the last thing he needed.

"Damon's still pissed at you, you know," the bear shifter said. "But I knew there was more to the story."

Anders crossed his arms over his chest. Back when Damon's mate, Anna Victoria, showed up at The Den and got drunk as a skunk on tequila, he had planned to help her out before anyone took advantage of her. However, Damon got to her first, then there was a fight with some anti-shifter assholes, but everything worked out anyway. Turns out Damon and Anna Victoria were mates and now they were married. Anna Victoria would probably be knocked up soon and they could live happily ever fucking after.

And if Damon thought Anders was still a scumbag asshole, then ... *good.* It would only help his carefully cultivated reputation. "Whatever," he snorted. "But from what I heard, you used to be quite the ladies' man yourself, Sarge. Had your share of soldier bunnies, or so they say."

"A man can change," he said with a shrug.

"Not this man. Every heard of the saying, a tiger can't change his stripes?"

"I know what you're trying to do." Krieger's dark eyes bore into his. "It's what I'm trying to do too."

Anders huffed as he turned around and shut the door. "And what's that?"

"Be a better man."

His head snapped back up, and he spun around. But Krieger was gone.

Be a better man.

"Yeah, right." Anders guffawed. There was no being a better man. Being a terrible person meant no one would want to get to know him, to peel back what was on the surface. It meant no one could come close enough.

A moan from the inside of the car jarred him out of his thoughts. Carrie's forehead thudded against the window as she continued to snooze. With an audible huff, he walked over to the driver's side and got in. Grabbing the purse from her shoulder, he checked her ID for her address, then started the engine. Good thing she didn't live in a dorm but in an apartment complex not far from the university in the next town over. He'd drop her off, leave her a note to remind her of where she parked her car, then drive back home. It used to be, he'd go and check up on them afterwards, making sure they were okay, but after the Darlene incident, he'd stopped doing that. He didn't need crazy stalkers coming to his work, threatening to kill themselves if he didn't come out to talk to them. It had been good for his reputation, but talking her down from the ledge was more trouble than it was worth.

Since it was his night off, he should really get some rest before his evening shifts for the week began. But he knew even if he did manage to block out his thoughts and cravings for *her*, she'd follow him into his dreams.

As soon as he got back home, he walked past the front porch. He went straight toward the woods behind his home, shedding his clothes along the way so he could fully shift into his tiger form. He let it take over for now, because at least it gave his animal a sense of control, some freedom to act on its instincts. It should be enough to satisfy his tiger, because there was no way he was going to give in to its other baser instincts. This would have to be enough.

Twenty-two days. Five hours. Thirteen minutes.

His mind was constantly on *her*. Sometimes, in his weakest moments, he'd allow his thoughts to wander. Who was she? Where did she come from? What was she doing at the reception? And where was she now?

———

That last question, of course, was constantly on Anders's mind. Where *was* she now?

He just never thought he'd get the answer on his way to work the next afternoon, as he gazed up at one of the many billboards along Highway 75.

"What the fuck?"

He slammed on the brakes, the seatbelt the only thing stopping his body from flying through his pickup's windshield. But he didn't feel the pain as the belt cut along his skin or heard the honks of the cars behind him nor see the angry faces and gestures of the drivers as they passed around him. No, he could only keep staring up. High up at the familiar lush lips, creamy skin, and aquamarine eyes as they stared down at him.

"Motherfucker!" His fists plowed forward, leaving a crack in the dash. Putting his car back into gear, he maneuvered onto the shoulder and cut the engine.

Pushing the door open, he attempted to slide out of the cab but the seatbelt held him back, choking him. "Goddammit!" He tugged and tugged until somehow his common sense came back, and he reached for the release and unbuckled himself.

Rounding to the front of his truck, he looked up, craning his neck back to get a good look at the fifty-foot billboard above him.

Fuck.

It was definitely her. Darcey Wednesday. Her blonde hair tumbled in soft waves around her, eyes heavily lidded as she lay on rumpled white sheets, wearing only a red lace corset. Sure, the photo was tastefully done and only showed her upper body, but she was still on display for everyone to see, her full breasts pushed up and her red lips parted. *Hot damn.* He was hard just looking up at her. And he was pretty sure every man over thirteen and under eighty passing by this stretch of highway would be too. His tiger roared possessively at that thought.

Mine!

If only he was a dragon, he could fly up there and burn the damned thing to ashes.

"Silk, Lace, and Whispers. Now open in South Blackstone," he managed to read aloud, once the haze of red cleared from his vision and he could see the copy scrawled at the bottom of the ad.

Darcey was some kind of model? *Of course she was*, he thought with a snort. She was gorgeous. A little on the short side, sure, but those curves were definitely made for silk and lace. And his hands roaming over her skin and ripping that delicate—

"Christ!" He spun on his heel and stomped back to his pickup, slamming the door so hard when he got in, the cab rattled. Rubbing his hands down his face, he started the truck, giving that damned billboard a quick glance, which was a big mistake because it didn't help his erection. He couldn't remember ever being so aroused and angry at the same time.

After checking the highway was clear, he got back on, speeding away from the billboard. Still, it was an image he couldn't erase from his mind, probably never would. Darcey on top of white silk sheets. Red lace covering her sweet body. Those plump lips, wondering how they would taste. How her body would feel under his.

Goddammit.

It was a fucking miracle he made it to HQ in one piece. His entire body was vibrating in anger—or need—he wasn't sure at this point because both emotions ebbed and flowed from him until he was a shaking mass of confusion.

He stalked into HQ, not bothering to return the greeting of his colleagues who were leaving for the day, or saying sorry to someone he bumped into.

"Excuse *me*," came the terse voice which was accompanied by a surly growl.

Whipping his head back, Anders could hardly suppress his tiger's annoyance at the sight of the tall man in gold-rimmed glasses. *This asshole.* Dr. What's-his-face. *Spenser,* he recalled. Damon had introduced him a few weeks back, and his superior attitude and stupid accent had rubbed Anders the wrong way. Spenser was supposed to be a ranger, but when he wasn't on patrol, preferred to hole himself up in his office, doing research or whatever bullshit he came here for.

"Sorry," Anders said in his most insincere tone, then dashed away. Entering the changing room, he headed straight to his locker to get into his uniform. As he slipped his shirt off, a loud, angry clang of a locker door slamming from behind caught his attention.

It was Daniel Rogers, fucking hero of Blackstone. However instead of his usual friendly smile, Rogers sent him a seething look, then headed toward the door, but not before he could feel the other man's bear roar at him in rage.

What the hell was with people and their animals today?

Wait. Rogers would know where Darcey was. "Hey, Rogers! Hold on!" Shutting his locker, he was about to chase after the other man when a snippet of conversation caught his sensitive hearing.

"... holy fuck, man, I'd like to get her between my sheets."

"Shit, I nearly swerved off the highway when I saw that billboard," someone said with a chuckle. "Woulda been worth it, though."

"Really? Then take a look at this."

There were several gasps. "Where'd you get that?"

"I want one."

"Fuck, I want two!"

Anders's shoulders tensed as he stalked around to the other row of lockers. Sure enough, a group of four guys from the day shift were gathered together.

"What the hell is going on here?" He pushed two of them aside. "What do you—" Fury rose in him, and the edges of his vision turned dark red. Sure enough, there was a postcard-sized version of Darcey's billboard on the inside of one of the lockers.

"Bro!" The owner of said locker, Davis—who had only passed the training course last year—called. "Have you seen this hottie?"

"Where did you get this?" he asked, his tone tense.

Davis chuckled. "I was out with my nephews and sister last Saturday in South Blackstone, and then I come across this lingerie shop, right? I stopped cuz that picture was displayed in the window, and when I peek inside—holy shit, *she* was in there, working the register! I go in—I don't care that it's all girly lacy underwear and shit—and I go up to her and chat her up a bit." A dark brow went up. "Lemme tell you, she's even hotter up close. Anyway, I chat her up, and I find out her name is Darcey, and she's not just the model, but the manager of the shop too. They had a whole rack of those post cards"—he nodded at the one hanging on his locker—"so I got one and even asked her to autograph it."

"She works here? In Blackstone?" one of the other guys—Gilmore—asked.

"Yeah." Davis smirked. "Maybe I'll head over there on my day off and—"

"You fucking better not!" Anders roared as he grabbed the postcard off the wall and tore it in half.

"What the fuck, bro?" Davis cried. "The hell are you—ack!"

Before he could stop himself, Anders had his hands around Davis's neck. "You stay the fuck away from her, if you know what's good for you!" He bared his teeth at the other men and growled.

"What the hell, man?" Gilmore cried. "What's the matter with you? You're choking him."

Turning back to Davis, he saw the other man's face turning purple. Shock made him relax his fingers. "Fuck," he spat. "Jesus, I—" Quickly, he did an about face and stomped to his locker, grabbing his uniform shirt and stormed out the door.

What the fuck just happened? Scrubbing a hand down his face, he let out a growl. She was still here, in Blackstone. Worked here, probably lived here too. Glancing down at the torn postcard in his hand, he saw the address of the lingerie shop.

"Don't even think about it," he told himself. His inner tiger, however, snarled at him and raked its claws down his insides. "Stop, I'm not going anywhere near her!" Stuffing the postcard pieces in his pocket, he put his shirt on and stalked off to begin his shift. Somehow, someway, he'd get Darcey Wednesday out of his system for good.

Chapter 3

"You have everything?" Sarah asked. "Lipstick? Wallet? Car keys? House keys?"

Darcey rolled her eyes. "Yes, *Mom*."

"Protection?" Sarah said with a brow raised.

"Ew, Sarah, it's only the second date," she admonished. And no, she didn't bring protection because she took her birth control religiously and even made an appointment with a new doctor in town to have her prescription switched here. Besides, she was a shifter, which meant she couldn't get any STDs. "I'm waiting for at least the third date for *that*."

"Ah, going the traditional route, are we?" Sarah teased. "Then how come he's not picking you up?"

"Because we haven't talked about my living situation yet," Darcey began. "I mean, don't get me wrong, I love living here—rent free, I may add—with you and Daniel and Adam, but I don't want to scare the guy away until I can figure out how he feels about that."

It wasn't that she was ashamed of her living situation, but it was definitely unique. Though she'd often thought about moving out, she didn't want to leave Adam or have Sarah and Daniel care for him all the time. Her brother was independent enough, but still needed help with transportation, plus, he'd always had her around, and she didn't want to change things too much for him. She figured that when Adam went off to college in two years, she could re-examine that situation, but for now, she was staying put.

"All right." Sarah hugged her. "You look gorgeous. Good luck. And have fun."

"I will. See you later." She made her way out the door, waving goodbye to Sarah as she got into her car. Excitement thrummed through her, but she did her best to tamp it down. *It's just a second date*, she told herself as she pulled out of the driveway and made her way toward Main Street.

Of course, she reasoned that anyone would be excited, given that her last two dates had been disasters. The first guy, someone J.D. had set her up with, was polite and nice, but so boring that she nearly fell asleep halfway through their date.

The second guy was the photographer who did the campaign for the shop, Jarrod McKlinskey. She liked Jarrod enough during the shoot, but he turned out to be a real creep. First, he ordered for her during their date without asking. Next, their conversations started normal, but then he started spouting sexist nonsense about how woman should stay at home, barefoot and pregnant in the kitchen before the salads even arrived. Darcey had been too shocked to leave right then and there, but when the waiter came to ask if they wanted dessert, she immediately made an excuse and left.

As if that wasn't bad enough, he kept texting her, and so she politely told him that she didn't feel a connection and they should just part ways. He replied by calling her a whore and bitch, and that *when*—not if—they went on their second date, he'd prove to her that they were meant to be together. She promptly blocked him after that, then started rethinking her plan.

Was there something about her deciding to stop chasing after unavailable men that the universe now only sent her jackasses and creeps? Or had she just always attracted the terrible men and she hadn't noticed?

Needless to say, she had been ready to give up—until she met Cam. Dr. Cameron Spenser. She had stopped by the coffee shop on Friday morning before work to grab her usual cup when she realized that her wallet was in the car. As she was explaining to the annoyed cashier that she'd come back, the person in line behind her offered to pay. Startled, she looked back at the gorgeous, tall man in the gold-rimmed glasses and an English accent that turned her brain to mush. Though she tried to say no, he insisted, and they ended up sitting together for a few minutes, chatting, and then exchanged numbers. It wasn't even lunchtime by the time he called, and they made a date for Saturday night. He took her to a French restaurant in South Blackstone, and Darcey had enjoyed herself so much that she agreed to a second date.

Calm yourself, she said. Her instinct would be to go all in, head over heels for this guy. And really, it was tempting. Cam was smart, polite, and had just enough aloofness that *of course* her first impulse was to make him want her and pay attention to her.

But that was the Old Darcey.

The New Darcey was going to play it cool. No mooning over him, imagining their future together or texting or calling him except to confirm the time and place of their second date. No, she had her feet firmly on the ground and her heart caged in her chest.

Her swan sighed sadly and hung its head down.

"None of that either," she admonished, maneuvering the car into the parking lot. Oh, she knew what the swan wanted. Or rather, who. But her chest twinged with pain each time she even thought about *him*. And so, she devoted much of her time to *not* thinking about him.

She slipped out of her car, shut the door, and smoothed her red dress down. It was tight enough to show off her curves, yet wasn't overly sexy. After checking her lipstick in the side-view mirror, she spun around and headed toward the entrance to Giorgio's, the local Italian eatery.

A strange feeling made her freeze. It was like every hair on her body stood up, and for the first time in three weeks, her swan jerked its head and swung around. Her shifter instinct was going haywire, and it was telling her something was wrong. But there was no one around, so her human brain told her she was being silly. But then again, it wasn't the first time she'd been approached by strangers lurking about.

It's that damned billboard. "Ugh." She slapped a palm on her forehead. *Why did I let J.D. convince me to pose for those pictures?* Perhaps it was the ten bottles of wine they finished off that made her say yes.

It sounded like a good idea at the time—get all glammed up, wear some of the lingerie Sarah designed, and have pictures taken for the store. They saved money by not hiring a professional model. Of course, she had no idea they were actually going to have a fifty-foot tall billboard of her on the most high-traffic section of the highway.

It had only been out for over a week, but since then, she's attracted a lot of attention, not just on social media, but guys coming up to her in the store or while she was out and about at the supermarket or at the cafe. If they hadn't paid upfront for the three months of the billboard-space, she would have insisted they take it down.

Of course, a small part of her couldn't even believe that was her on the billboard. Jarrod had been a creep, but he was a damned talented photographer. The photo had turned out classy and sensual, and not dirty or cheap. The campaign had also caused a surge in traffic and sales which she was happy for.

Yes, that had to be it. She was being paranoid. Brushing off the feeling, she dashed into the restaurant. To her relief, Cam was already by the host's station, looking handsome in his suit, his hair tied back in a ponytail, gold-rimmed glasses perched on his aquiline nose. He smiled when he saw her, though his light, blue-violet eyes remained flat.

He was a shifter, of course, but what, she wasn't sure. Of course, she'd told him what she was back on their first date, even though he didn't offer to tell her his own animal, and she hadn't asked because it seemed impolite. But she could tell he was something big and ... cold? There was something about him that felt unreachable, like a part of him that was encased in ice.

"Good evening, Darcey. You look gorgeous," he said, his accent making her all giddy.

"Thank you, Cam. So do you. I mean, you look great," she said nervously, wondering if Cam had seen the billboard, and if so, how did he react? Would he get all jealous and not want to go out with her anymore? Or would he think she was some easy tramp and try to coax her into bed tonight?

"These are for you." He swung his arm around and lifted an arrangement of flowers he'd been hiding behind him.

"Oh, Cam." Her eyes went wide as she accepted the half dozen red roses wrapped up in tissue. "These are beautiful." Closing her eyes, she took a whiff. "And they smell good too." She flashed him a dazzling smile, waiting for a reaction from her body. Like her stomach flipping or her heart thudding faster.

But there was nothing. Nothing except the sad huff from her swan. It didn't even ask the usual question it did whenever she met a guy. She almost missed the way it would cry out —*mine?*

Old Darcey, she reminded herself. "Thank you for bringing these."

Cam turned to the host. "Do you have our table ready?"

"Of course, sir," the young man said. "Follow me."

They sat down at their table, chatted as they looked over the menu and ordered, and generally enjoyed themselves over the delicious Italian food. They lingered over coffee and dessert, and though Darcey found herself having a good time, there was something that just didn't feel right.

Cam was handsome, attentive, and smart. He was some kind of researcher and was technically a doctor. "Not that kind of doctor," he had said last week on their first date, but rather, he studied animals and plants, which was why he moved to Blackstone from England. All he ever talked about was work or books and articles he read. Not that she was bored, but he never talked about himself or his family at all. Sure, she talked about her own work and her life back in Las Vegas and what it was like moving here, but also, she dropped hints about her own family life, mentioning Adam and Sarah and Daniel, but he didn't seem to pick up on it, keeping mum about his own personal life.

By the time the waiter was clearing their cups and dessert plates, Darcey felt drained. Sadly, though she had been excited at the beginning of the night, it was hard to muster up any more attraction or interest in him. In a way, that was a good thing, because that meant she was putting Old Darcey aside, not immediately going all in with a guy. But still, she couldn't help feeling there was more than that.

"Can I give you some cash for that?" she said when Cam reached for the folder on the table.

Cam slipped a black card into the folder, then handed it to a passing waiter. "I invited you, so I should pay," he said. "I insist."

"Thank you." She only hoped Cam wouldn't ask her out again, or worse—ask her to come back to his place or head to hers. She cleared her throat and was about to say something when he spoke first.

"I had a lovely time tonight, Darcey," he began. "Unfortunately, I have an early day tomorrow."

Relief poured through her. "You do?"

He nodded. "There's a species of grouse I've been meaning to catalogue, and according to my research I may be able to observe it on the northeast side of the mountain. I need to get up early and hike up there before anyone else arrives."

"Oh, how uh, exciting."

"Excuse me, sir," their waiter interrupted. "We're having some trouble with your card. Would you mind coming up to the machine, or do you have another form of payment?"

Cam frowned. "Of course, but why don't we try that card again? Otherwise, I do have some cash. Will you excuse me for a moment, Darcey?"

"Actually, if you don't mind, I'd like to head out." She let out a yawn. "I have an early day tomorrow, too, since it's inventory day."

"I can walk you out, if you can give me a minute."

"No, it's fine, sort out your card." She got to her feet and slung her purse over her shoulder.

"I'll call you."

"Sure," she replied automatically. Maybe she could let him down easier over a phone call. This was only a second date after all. "Goodnight, Cam. Thanks for the meal."

Heading toward the exit, she stepped out into the cool evening. It was so different here in the mountains, so unlike the dry desert air of the Nevada. Still, the stiff breeze shouldn't have been enough to send an icy, prickly sensation down her spine, especially not with her shifter ability to adjust to extreme temperature. Her inner animal went on alert again, much like it did earlier, as if someone was watching her. *I should have had Cam walk me back.*

Her heart pounded in her chest as she scampered back to her car, her stiletto heels clicking across the concrete. She dug through her purse, cursing herself for not taking her keys out first before leaving the restaurant. Living in Blackstone had made her feel too safe. Finally, she found them in her purse and clicked the unlock button, but as she reached for the handle, she froze when she heard someone's voice behind her.

"You look nice."

What the hell?

She sucked in a breath. Her skin tingled—this time for a different reason. Though she had only heard that low baritone once, she instantly recognized it. Her stomach flipped, and her swan twittered excitedly.

Mine. Mine. Mine.

Gritting her teeth, she turned around slowly. The impact of his presence made her traitorous little heart nearly burst out of her chest. "W-what are you doing here?"

Anders's golden eyes flashed, and his lips curled up into a smile. "What, I can't have dinner out on Main Street? I've lived in Blackstone all my life, darling. Can't say the same for you."

Her nostrils flared. "I live here now, too, and last I heard, it's a free country. Goodnight." She turned back to her car and opened the door. However, a hand reached out over her shoulder and slammed it shut. The warmth of his body, so close to hers but not quite touching, made her knees wobble. "What the hell are you doing?" She hadn't meant for that to come out so breathy and sensual.

"Why'd you leave your date inside? You guys seemed like you were having a good time. Didn't see his face, though. Who is he?"

Jesus, was he following her? All this time? Was that why she felt like she was being watched?

Her instinct—and her swan, too—was telling her it couldn't be him making her feel unsafe. If anything, his presence now made that initial fear melt away.

Stop it! That's Old Darcey talking.

"Why are you following me?" she said. "Have you been watching me on all my dates?"

He huffed, sending the warm puff of his breath across the skin of her neck. "*All* your dates? So, this isn't the first one? Exactly how many guys have you been dating? Have you fucked any of them and—"

"Screw you, Anders!" She whirled around and planted her palms on his broad chest, pushing him away with a strength she didn't know she had. He staggered back, a shocked look on his face because obviously, he didn't know she had it in her either. "Y-you told me to stay away from you, and that's what I've been doing. So if you could please do me the courtesy of doing the same, I'd appreciate it."

"You've been staying away from me?" he scoffed. "How the fuck is being on my Goddamn commute every day, fifty-feet tall, and staring down at me with your tits hanging out 'staying away'? Or when you're on every fucking locker at HQ. My piece of shit coworkers are probably jerking off to—"

"What's going on here?"

Cam! "N-nothing," she stammered, taking a step away from Anders. "I thought you were sorting out your card."

Cam stood behind Anders, the bouquet of flowers in his

hand. "I was, but you forgot these."

Anders's face turned red as he slowly pivoted on his heel. "Jesus *fucking* Christ, you were on a date with *this* guy?"

Cam's eyes glowed like twin blue-violet fires, magnified by the glass in front of them. "Something the matter, Stevens?"

Anders's mouth opened, but he shut it quickly. "Nothing. At all." He snorted and waved his hand dismissively, then stormed off into the street, melting into the darkness.

"Are you all right?" Cam asked, his voice soothing like ice on a burn.

"I-I'm fine," she stammered. "Thanks. Sorry I forgot about the roses." As she took the flowers from him, she could see that he was hesitating, like he wanted to ask about Anders. And to be honest she wanted him to, so she could confess to him what she'd been keeping close to her chest. Maybe even get some sympathy.

But no, that layer of cool aloofness came over Cam, and he gave her a nod. "Goodnight then. I'll speak with you soon."

"Goodnight, Cam," she called softly as he walked away. Getting into her car, she placed the flowers on the passenger seat and shut her door.

Now that she was alone, Anders's words came back to her. They had hit her, deep. So, he'd seen the billboard. Of course he had. Frankly, he was the last person on her mind when she'd agreed to do that photoshoot. In fact, she didn't even expect him to react, much less seek her out to berate her.

She reached up to cover her face with her hands, but then pulled them away. "I will not be slut-shamed." Especially not by that man-whoring asshole. With a determined grunt, she started the engine, vowing to put Anders behind her. Checking her rearview mirror, she looked up at her own reflection.

"You're the New Darcey now," she reminded herself. And the New Darcey would be here to stay.

———

Darcey stretched her arms over her head and closed her tired, dry eyes. When she opened them again, she glanced at the clock on her computer screen. It was almost ten o'clock in the evening. She had closed up the boutique at six thirty, took a short dinner break, and went into the back office, which meant she'd been hunched over the computer for over three hours non-stop.

There was a ton of work to be done which was why she elected to stay late and have Sarah go home and make dinner for Adam. Retail work was not just about selling and being with customers, but there was a lot of stuff going on behind the scenes, especially now that she was actually part owner. Inventory, accounting, payroll, marketing, advertising—there were many hats she had to wear now. Though she hated this part of the work, she was glad as it served as a good distraction for her.

It had been a few days since that night when Anders had popped out of nowhere, and her emotions were still a mess, swinging from elation from actually seeing him again to anger at his audacity. Did he really follow her around, just to berate her for that billboard? Was he actually jealous? Of the guys seeing her and of *Cam*?

She glanced guiltily at her phone which was on the desk beside her placed in silent mode. When she saw Cam's name pop up, she let it go to voicemail. She couldn't bring herself to call him back yet. He would probably ask her out again, but she didn't know what to say. It wasn't that she didn't like him, it was just ... she didn't feel anything for him at all. And it annoyed the heck out of her that here was this gorgeous, single man asking her out, yet she was focused on some asshole who didn't even want her.

Her swan huffed and hung its neck down.

"Whatever." Pushing her chair back, she got up, turned the computer off, then grabbed her phone and purse. *Time to go home.* Sarah had messaged earlier saying that Daniel had to stay late because of an emergency at work. If he wasn't home yet, then maybe she and Sarah could have a glass of wine and have some girl time. Or they could coax Adam into watching a movie with them, after all, it had been a while since just the three of them hung out.

As she walked out into the darkened boutique, she stopped short. The sound of glass breaking made her heart stop, and her swan suddenly went on alert, letting out a loud hiss and raising its wings.

A scream ripped from her mouth as something slammed against her, throwing her down to the floor. She tried to scream again, but a hand covered her mouth. Someone large and heavy was pinning her down, pushing her head to the side. Her skin crawled as she felt her attacker press his nose to her neck and inhale deeply.

Tears pricked at her eyes as she was hauled up to her feet, then dragged across the carpeted floor of the shop toward the exit. Her swan honked angrily, flapping its wings as if saying, *fight, damn you.*

With a sharp cry, Darcey yanked her wrists back. It must have surprised her attacker because he shouted and let go. Hope soared in her, but he recovered quickly, making a grab for her. He managed to grab her shirt and haul her forward, slamming a palm into her face.

Her swan squawked in fury as pain exploded in her cheek. Her skin prickled as she felt the sharp needles of her wings pushing through her arms. *Oh no!* She was going to shift.

Reaching out with her hands, she managed to claw at him, but he pulled hard, spun them around and sent them sailing forward. Glass shattered around them as they went through the window and landed outside the shop.

"Help!" Darcey cried as she rolled away from her attacker, not caring that bits of glass dug into her face and sliced her skin. Something behind her shuffled, and she heard the sound of footsteps racing away from her. Gingerly, she turned her head.

He was gone.

Her swan retreated, and the skin on her arms returned to normal as the tips of her feathers retracted. Unfortunately, that left her vulnerable, and more glass cut into her. She winced in pain as she got up, carefully brushing the debris from her hair and clothes, pulling out the larger pieces lodged in her skin. Her shoulder felt like it was on fire, but she managed to stand up straight.

Footsteps coming toward her made her go on alert again, but she relaxed when she recognized the barista from the cafe a few doors down.

"Miss!" the young woman shouted. "Are you all right? What happened?"

"I ... I ..." She bit her lip to keep from crying. "Someone ... someone broke in." She nodded at what was left of the window. The glass door, too, had been shattered. *Probably how he got inside.*

"I'll call the police," the barista said. "Do you want to call someone? Family? You can wait in the cafe if you want."

She nodded and bent down to reach for her purse which had fallen off her shoulder. Reaching inside, she grabbed her phone and dialed Sarah's number with shaky hands. *Busy.* Right. She said she was going to be on a long conference call with a new supplier from Taiwan. But who else could she call? Not Adam. Who else—

She worried at her lip and scrolled through her contacts,

tapping the name she had been searching for. The only other person she trusted in this town. He picked up on the first ring.

"Darcey?" Daniel asked.

Relief made tears spring to her eyes. "Daniel," she sobbed. "Can you come to the shop? Something's happened."

Chapter 4

Most evenings working the night shift were pretty boring, which was one of the reasons Anders worked it as much as he could. There were other reasons, too, reasons he would never tell anyone, but if any of his coworkers ever found out the truth well ... well, he would rather walk over hot nails and coal than have them find out about his daytime "activities."

But other times, the evening shift could be exciting. And tonight, well, it was a clusterfuck. Exciting, but a clusterfuck nonetheless. Anders had barely gotten through the door to start his shift when all-hands-on-deck were called up in sector 5-H. Apparently, a couple of juvenile bear shifters had run into a bunch of smaller shifters burrowing around a clearing. The teens thought it would be a great idea to scare the living shit out of them by charging in, but they didn't realize that they were about to tangle with a company of honey badger shifters.

Though the bears were much larger, the mature honey badgers didn't back down and well ... everyone ended up scratched and wounded, and two of the teens had to be airlifted down to Blackstone Hospital.

And here they were, the six rangers idiotic enough to get in the middle of a fight where honey badgers were involved, worse for wear, squeezed into the truck bed of the transport truck. They were headed back to HQ so they could debrief with the chief. They were bumping along down the road that led there, when Anders decided to break the silence.

"So, honey badgers *really* don't give a shit, *amiright*?"

Everyone in the truck looked at each other's bruised and scratched faces, then laughed. Well, everyone except for one person—Daniel Rogers, sitting near the edge. His jaw set and his eyes turned to steel before they turned away, looking out into the darkness.

"Can't win 'em all," Anders muttered. But then again, Rogers had been giving him the cold shoulder for days now.

He shrugged. It really shouldn't bother him. Rogers had always been the good guy, the one everyone could depend on. Sure, he was quiet and never said a bad word or acted self-righteous, but sometimes, he just rubbed Anders the wrong way. So, when the truck stopped and Rogers hopped out of the truck, Anders decided he wasn't going to stand back anymore.

"Yo, Rogers, you got a problem with me or something?" he said as he caught up to the other man, using his speed to get in front of him.

The bear shifter sent him a glare then sidestepped. But Anders wasn't going to let him get away that easy. He blocked him again. "Look, if you got a problem with me, then be a man and say it to my face. Stop acting like some girl on her period, giving me the stink eye from afar."

Daniel let out a huff. "Just leave me alone, okay, Stevens?"

Anders grit his teeth. "Not when you're treating me like I got the plague and you're acting like a jerk."

Daniel's eyes blazed. "Me? I'm the jerk?" he growled. "Get your head out of your ass and look in the mirror."

Anders could feel the other man's animal roar at him. His

tiger didn't back down, however, as it rolled its shoulders, twisted its ears, and lashed its tail. "Just tell me what the fuck is going on with you." The truth was, though Anders did his best not to get close to anyone, he kinda thought he and Daniel were, well, friends. The two of them, along with Damon, Gabriel, and Krieger had gone through the rangers training together five years ago, and though they weren't all the best of buds, that kind of thing was enough to forge a bond.

"God, you don't even know. Don't even care." Daniel's lips twisted.

"About what?"

The bear shifter's eyes glowed briefly. "Darcey."

Anders sucked in a breath. "You know." Of course he did. "What do you care anyway?" he huffed. "Aren't you already happily married? Or is your Mrs. already old news and you're looking to stray—"

"Fuck you!" Daniel grabbed him by the collar. "You selfish asshole! Why the hell would I even think of my sister-in-law that way?"

Jesus. "Sister-in-law?"

"Yeah. She's Sarah's sister."

"Sister?" he repeated. Geez, he was starting to sound like a parrot. "I thought Sarah's last name was Mendez?" He remembered reading about it in the newspapers when it was first discovered she and Daniel had been married all along.

"She's adopted. They all are," Daniel groused. "Which means Darcey's happiness is my business. She's my family. Under *my* protection."

His tiger did not like that last part at all and let out a protesting roar. *Mine.* "You—"

A ringing sound interrupted them, making Daniel let go and reach into his uniform breast pocket for his phone. Glancing at the screen, he frowned and picked up. "Darcey?"

Anders's tiger perked up at the sound of the name, and he couldn't stop his heart from skipping a beat. But why would she be calling Daniel? As the expression on the other man's face darkened, a pit began to form in his stomach.

"Stay there," Daniel murmured, though the grip on his phone tightened, as evidenced by the way his knuckles turned white. "I'll be there as soon as I can." Putting his phone away, he turned on his heel and strode away.

"Hey!" Anders called. "That was Darcey? What did she want?"

"Fuck off, Stevens," Daniel growled. "This is none of your business."

"If this is about Darcey, then—"

"I said, it's none of your business!" Daniel bared his teeth, the incisors enlarging as he let out an inhuman roar. His eyes blazed with fury, but before he could act on it, he strode off.

Anders stood there, stunned. Slowly, though, a feeling of dread came over him. Something was wrong. And Darcey was somehow caught in it.

Without thinking, he dashed after Daniel. He saw him get into his truck, so Anders did the same, bolting toward his own pickup to chase after Daniel.

There was only one road down the mountains, so it wasn't hard to keep up with the bear shifter. It was, however, a long ride, even longer than the usual forty-five minutes as various scenarios came up in his head of what could have happened. Was she hurt? Or in trouble? Was she safe?

He forced himself to calm down. It was probably Sarah. While he didn't wish Daniel's mate harm, he could only imagine that the reason Daniel would go tearing down the mountain like this was because of her.

As they reached the town, Daniel made a left turn on Main Street, which meant he was heading toward South Blackstone.

Where could he be going? Minutes later, he got his answer as Daniel parked in front of the row of retail shops and restaurants in the trendy entertainment district. Anders stopped his truck behind him and followed as he headed toward the shops.

At this time of night, it should have been dark and quiet, but the flashing lights of a parked cop car projected blue and red across the unlit row of buildings. Beside the police vehicle, the EMT med-van made the scene even more ominous.

Ignoring the ice building in his stomach, he walked onward keeping his eye on Daniel as he ran down a row of shops. He stopped for a second in front of one of the stores, let out a curse before continuing onwards. When Anders caught up, he saw what had made Daniel swear aloud.

One of the shops had broken glass in front of it. It looked like the entire front window had been smashed. As he took a sniff, the smell of blood and something familiar tickled his nose. Feathers.

Fury boiled inside him. That was Darcey's blood. His tiger raged, slamming its head against his ribcage, roaring to get out. Frankly, he would have let it—except he had to know where the hell Darcey was, find out what happened, and kill the bastard who made her bleed.

Carefully stepping over the broken glass, he walked toward where Daniel had stalked off to. The only place open was a cafe, so he pushed the door open and checked inside.

"... look at what he did to her!" Sarah Mendez cried. "Daniel—"

"We'll take care of this, baby doll," Daniel soothed as he took his mate in his arms. "Don't you worry."

Anders quickly strode inside, his gaze zeroing in on the figure sitting on the couch, head down and hands folded in her lap. Beside her, he recognized Deputy Police Chief, Cole Carson, talking to her softly. The sight of an unmated male so close to her was enough to make his tiger snarl loudly, the sound rattling from his chest. Both of them looked up at him, but he ignored Carson. Instead he focused on Darcey's beautiful face, marred by a bruise on her cheek and various healing cuts all over her skin.

"Goddamned motherfucking sonofabitch!" Ignoring the protests directed at him, he bolted toward Darcey, kneeling in front of her. When he tried to reach out, she flinched away from him, and he cursed inwardly. "Who did this to you?" he demanded. "Tell me." *And he won't live to see tomorrow.*

"I-it's already healing," she whispered. "I'm fine."

"No, you're not," he growled. "Someone hurt you. Who was it?"

"Get away from her, you asshole!" Sarah shouted. "How dare you come in here?" She turned to Daniel. "How could you bring him here, after ... after ..."

"I didn't," Daniel put his hands up defensively. He shot Anders a dirty look.

"I want him to leave," Sarah barked at Carson.

"Now, now." Carson's voice was calm. "Let's all step back for a bit. We're here because someone attacked Ms. Wednesday." He glanced at Anders, one brow shooting up, then turned to Darcey. "Ma'am, you didn't want to come down to the station to make a statement, and I'm fine with that, I can take it here. But you really need to tell me what happened now while your memory is still fresh. Or we can still head to the station."

She nodded. "Here is fine."

Carson took out a notepad from his pocket, flipped it open, and pressed the tip of his pen to the page. "All right, start from the beginning."

"I was w-working late tonight, by myself, and I was about to go home...."

Anders slid onto the couch beside her, his entire body

growing tenser and tenser as Darcey began to tell them what happened. By the time she was done, he felt hot and flush with fury, and his tiger was chomping at the bit wanting to get out.

"... and then after I called Daniel, I was finally able reach Sarah and she came here," Darcey finished. "Th-that's about it, Deputy."

"Thank you so much, Ms. Wednesday, and I'm sorry about what happened. Are you sure you don't want to get checked out by an EMT? They're on standby outside."

She shook her head. "I-I-I'm all right. I think these"—she gestured to the bruises and cuts on her arms—"should be gone by morning."

"And thank you for letting me take pictures of them as evidence earlier," Carson said. "Is there anything else you can tell us? You said he didn't say anything? Just ... sniffed you?"

"Did he touch you?" Anders asked, hands curling into fists.

She scowled at him. "I told you, that's all he did. I mean, before he dragged me across the shop and I tried to get away and we went through the window."

"Could he have been trying to kidnap her?" Sarah asked.

"Maybe," Cole said. "Sounds like he was trying to identify you based on scent, and when he figured out what you were ..."

"Those damned anti-shifters," Daniel snarled.

"Wait, that doesn't make sense," Darcey said with a shake of her head. "He had to have been a shifter, too, right? If he sniffed me?"

"Was he a shifter, Ms. Wednesday?"

"Please, call me Darcey. And ..." She closed her eyes. "I think so. It was dark, and he knew where I was. And he was definitely strong. Strong as me anyway. But everything happened so fast so I couldn't tell what he was exactly."

Daniel rubbed his chin with his thumb and forefinger. "A stalker then?"

"It's that damned billboard." Anders could feel his blood pressure rising.

"Billboard?" Cole asked.

"Are you blind, Carson?" Anders curled his lips back distastefully. "The one on Seventy-Five where she's got her—"

"Stevens," Daniel warned. "You know the one, Cole. Right by exit seven."

Recognition flashed across the deputy's face, as well as a hint of lust, which only made Anders want to pound it in more. "Ah, yeah." The professional, emotionless mask slipped back on his face. "Have you gotten any extra attention since the billboard went up?"

Darcey cleared her throat. "There have been some guys coming up to me while I'm out or at the store ... being persistent," she said. "But I don't think they would do something like this. Maybe this was someone who wanted to rob us?"

"All good theories," Cole said as he put his notebook and pen away. "I need to check if my lab guys have arrived, then head back to the station and put the report in. I'll take your contact info before you go. Do you live alone? Do you have someone to stay with you?"

"She's with us," Daniel informed him. "She won't be alone."

"Good. If you'll excuse me." He tipped his hat and then stalked toward the door.

"Jesus." Anders raked his hand through his hair. "What the hell were you doing by yourself this late?" he said to Darcey. "What if that bastard succeeded in his plans? If he had gotten to you—"

"What do you care?" Darcey exploded, shooting to her feet. "Who asked you to come anyway? You have no right to be here."

The words stung because they were the truth. And he knew she was correct. He had no right to be here; he threw that away the moment he rejected her.

"Let's go home, Darce." Sarah placed herself between him and Darcey. "You should get some rest." Putting an arm around her sister, she led her away from him, and they left the coffee shop.

Anders made a motion to go after her, but Daniel blocked him, placing a hand on his shoulder. "Take your hands off me unless you don't want it back," he warned.

"Oh yeah?" Daniel challenged. "Just try it, Stevens."

He huffed, but didn't say a word.

"She's not your concern," Daniel warned. "You don't want to be her mate? That's fine. Your choice, no one can make you bond with her. But you stay away from her from now on. She doesn't need a piece of shit like you hanging around."

He just stood there, unmoving. Even when Daniel left and he was alone, he didn't move a muscle. Yeah, he was a piece of shit all right. Wasn't that what he wanted people to think? So they would never get close enough?

He couldn't risk it. Couldn't let anyone close enough to touch him, because everything that he came in contact with turned to shit. He'd ruined things all his life, and he would ruin *her* too.

And Daniel was right—Darcey didn't need a piece of shit like him. She was better off—everyone was better off without him. He shut his eyes, reminding himself of why.

Why did you have to spawn that brat?

He'll just grow up to be like his father. A boozer with no future.

He's ruining everything.

He was doing Darcey a favor by rejecting her. That thought repeated in his head like a mantra, and it would be best for everyone involved if he just stayed away from her.

Chapter 5

"I swear, Sarah, I'm fine." Darcey crossed her arms over her chest. "Will you guys please stop coddling me?"

"We're not." Sarah glanced over at Daniel.

"We're just concerned," Daniel added.

"Then why does this feel like an intervention?"

Daniel and Sarah were already in the kitchen when she came down at seven o'clock on the dot as she did every morning. Usually at this time, all three of them would have breakfast before Daniel went off to do his shift and she and Sarah headed off to the shop. They let Adam sleep in, since he was a teenager and it was the last few days of his summer vacation.

This morning, however, as she came down, all dressed and ready for work, Sarah had "suggested," i.e. told Darcey, that she should stay home.

"Someone tried to hurt you last night." Sarah's hands curled into fists at her sides. "You should stay here and rest."

"I'm all healed up." Darcey gestured at her arms and face, to show them that all the cuts and bruises were gone.

"The shop isn't cleaned up either," her sister added. "Daniel went back to cover up the broken window and door with a board, but the repair guys won't be coming by until lunch. We might not even open at all today."

"All the more reason I should come. You'll need help cleaning up."

"Ugh!" Sarah threw her hands up. "I'm going to wake up Adam." She looked to Daniel, and a silent communication seemed to pass between them before she pivoted on her heel and headed out of the kitchen.

"You know she's only like this because she cares about you," Daniel said.

"I know." With a sigh, she sank down on one of the kitchen chairs. "I'm telling you, I'm fine. Sure, I was a little rattled last night, but I'm all good now."

"We still don't know who attacked you," he pointed out. "He could come back."

"I'm sure he was just some guy looking for a couple of dollars."

"Blackstone doesn't have panhandlers or homeless people," he said. "We take care of our own here. What if Anders was right about the billboard?"

Her head snapped up. "Of all the sexist, chauvinistic—" She pressed her lips together. "Don't you slut-shame me too."

Daniel's eyes widened. "Darce, no, it's not like that." He sat down next to her. "I'm sorry. I didn't mean for it to come out that way. Of course, you're free to do what you want with your body. Sarah would skin me alive if I even thought ..." He took a deep breath. "And I'm sorry. About Anders."

It was difficult not to wince, or stop the glum feeling clouding over her. Her swan, too, whimpered at the mention of the name. It had been elated to see him last night and have him close. His presence soothed their nerves, which irritated the hell out of her.

"I didn't bring him there on purpose." Daniel had told her

that Anders happened to be right in front of him when she called.

"I believe you." She had trusted him enough to tell him what animal she was a few weeks ago, so she trusted him to tell her the truth. "I still don't understand, though, why did he come all the way down?"

Daniel sent her a sympathetic look. "I know you grew up without anyone to explain the mate thing to you, but I hope I can try," he began. "See, as your mate, Anders is always going to feel a connection to you. It's his protective instinct. And you probably still feel drawn to him, too, at least your swan is."

A hand went up to her chest. She was always going to feel this way? "How ... how can I stop it? Is there a way for us to not be mates?"

Daniel shook his head. "I don't know. I only know what my parents told me. But, as long as you don't bond, the mating should remain incomplete. It's not the end of the world, Darcey," he assured her. "My mom had me, and she and my dad weren't mates. They were happy together too. You can still find someone else and have a family with them."

Her swan flapped its wings in protest. "I ... thanks, Daniel." That gave her some hope.

"Ugh, why am I waking up so early?"

She turned toward the doorway, where Sarah pushed Adam in as the teen rubbed his eyes. Darcey had asked Daniel and Sarah not to tell him about the attack, but only that there had been a break-in at the store.

"Seven twenty is not early," Sarah said. "Besides, you should start waking up at this time, so you can get used to it when school starts."

"Yeah, yeah." He rolled over to Darcey. "So, Sarah tells me that you're playing hooky at work today, and we should do something together."

"I am, am I?" She shot her sister a dirty look. Sarah could be pretty sneaky when she wanted to. But ... it was a day off, and she would get to spend time with Adam, which she hadn't done since she had gotten back from Vegas. "Sure. What do you want to do? Watch a movie? Pie at Rosie's? Hiking? Computer store?"

"I've been hanging around town doing all those things for weeks," he said. "Why don't we do something different? What do you want to do?"

Darcey tapped a finger on her chin. "I'm not sure either." Back in Vegas when she worked at a children's clothing boutique, she hardly had any time off. Her witch of a boss, Agnes, had her at the shop from morning until night. On her days off, she caught up with housework, then scrolled through her dating apps or scheduled a date. Seeing as she was definitely not doing those last two and Adam wouldn't want to spend the day cleaning the house, she would have to think of something else.

"Darcey," Sarah began. "You used to go back and visit the orphanage where you lived, right?"

She nodded. "Every couple of months." On the rare times she did have two consecutive days off, she made the three-hour drive up to St. Margaret's in Lund to visit the sisters and bring treats for the kids. It was too bad that now that she lived in Colorado, her visits would become even rarer, though she did vow that once she saved up enough money, she'd go back again.

"Maybe you guys could look into doing some volunteer work," Sarah suggested. "Daniel, is there something like that around here? A senior center, food bank, orphanage, or shelter of some kind?"

Daniels blond brows knit together. "*Hmm.* I'm not sure, actually. See, the Lennox Foundation pretty much takes care of everyone here. School, healthcare, and most things people around here need. Maybe Jason—he's the head of Lennox

Foundation—might have something, but as far as I know, they work with paid staff and don't really need volunteers."

"If everyone around here's taken care of, why would they need our help?" Adam pointed out. "Maybe we should look outside of town."

"That's a great idea, Adam." Perhaps thinking about something other than her own problems would help distract her and put things in perspective.

"It might be a great opportunity for you, too, Adam," Daniel added. "Something to add to your college application."

"Great!" Adam said. "I'll start looking."

———

Darcey and Adam searched for any kind of volunteer opportunities in the nearby towns. Eventually, they found something that wasn't too far out—just thirty minutes from where they were, in a town called Greenville. There was a community center there that catered to kids from low-income families and offered before and after school programs as well as support for parents. They called up the center and were told that, yes, they were in need of volunteers, and they could visit that afternoon.

Later that day, they headed to the Greenville Community Center. The building itself was obviously a few decades old, but it was clean and well-kept. The bright yellow and white paint added a cheerful, welcoming look.

"Hello," she greeted the older, white-haired woman at the reception area when she walked in. "I'm Darcey. Darcey Wednesday."

"Oh." The woman smiled and clapped her hands together. "Darcey! Welcome. I'm Betty. We spoke over the phone."

Circling around the reception desk, she shuffled over and offered her hand.

Darcey shook it. "Nice to meet you, Betty." She stepped aside to let Adam in. "This is my brother, Adam."

Betty offered her hand to Adam. "Lovely to meet you, Adam."

"Thanks," he said, shaking the older woman's hand. "Nice to meet you too."

"Welcome to Greenville Community Center," Betty said warmly. "I'm so glad you're interested in joining us."

"We're glad to be here," Darcey replied. "Where do we start?"

"Why don't I take you on a quick tour?" Betty suggested. "We're not a huge center like the one in Verona Mills, so it won't take too long. We can also chat along the way, and you can tell me what you were thinking of in terms of volunteering with us."

Betty led them down the hallway from the reception area, taking them to the cramped offices, a small indoor play area, study room, kitchen, and the lunchroom.

"And now," Betty began as they walked down the long corridor, "let's head into the gym. Actually, it's more of a multipurpose hall, and frankly, it's not like those fancy high school gymnasiums, but sports are our most popular programs." She pushed on the double doors at the end of the hallway. "Oh, you're just in time too. We have our karate class going on."

Coordinated shouts and the sound of feet slapping on the floor greeted them as they entered the gym. Betty was right—it wasn't much of a gym, and it was obviously the most used area of the community center. The concrete bleachers were a drab gray, the paint on the wall was peeling, and the hardwood floors had seen better days.

In the middle of the gym, a group of about fifteen kids of varying ages wearing white uniforms were lined up in a grid atop rubber mats. They moved in sync as they went through a series of kicks and punches. At the front of the class was a tall man dressed in a white top and pants, a black belt tied around his waist.

Darcey's skin prickled involuntarily, making her frown. Where the heck had that come from? As the man turned his head, she realized why she'd reacted that way.

Mine! Her swan flapped its wings happily.

Anders? What was *he* doing *here?*

"Darcey?" Adam asked. "You okay?"

She blinked. Betty and Adam were already a few steps ahead of her, while she remained rooted to the spot. Shock and awareness coursed through her, making it hard to breathe.

Betty cocked her head toward the class. "Come, I'll introduce you to the kids and Sensei Stevens."

Sensei Stevens?

Her swan urged her forward, and it was as if she had no choice. As she drew closer to him, her heart hammered a quick rhythm in her chest.

Anders put his hand up and the class stopped. "Great job, everyone. Water break." The kids scattered off, most of them making a beeline for the water fountain in the corner. Stepping forward, Anders knelt down in front of one of the students—a little girl, probably no more than six or seven, who was also the smallest of the class.

"See, Janine?" he said, in a patient voice. "I told you, you could finish the entire *kata*. Did you practice at home like I told you?"

The girl's face lit up, and her mouth spread into a grin, revealing missing front teeth. "I have, Sensei," she lisped. "Every day."

He ruffled her curly mop of hair affectionately. "Good. If you keep it up, you'll only get better, I promise. Now go and get some water before we start again." Janine flashed him another smile before she ran off to join her classmates.

"Sensei Stevens!" Betty called. "We have some visitors here."

As Anders got up, Darcey fought the urge to run and hide. Her swan didn't like that at all, and pecked at her to stay there.

"Hey, Betty," Anders greeted as he got up and turned. "Who are—Darcey?" Surprise flashed across this face as his jaw dropped.

Darcey swallowed hard as her stomach flip-flopped. "Anders."

"Oh." Betty's gaze went from Anders to Darcey and back again. "I didn't realize you knew each other already."

"Who is this guy?" Adam asked, eyeing Anders suspiciously.

"H-he works with Daniel," Darcey managed to say. "Our brother-in-law," she explained to Betty.

"How lovely that you're already acquainted," Betty said.

"What are they doing here?" Anders asked, his gaze never leaving hers.

"I'm taking them on a tour," Betty explained. "They want to volunteer here."

His lips pressed together. "That's nice."

She bristled at his tone, because it was obvious he wasn't crazy about them being here. Or at least, her.

"I should get back to my students," he said curtly.

"Of course, Sensei," Betty said. "You have about fifteen minutes left, right? We'll just stay on the sidelines and watch the rest of your class, then we can all head to the lunchroom for snacks. Maybe you can tell Darcey and Adam more about volunteering here."

He nodded and pivoted, clapping his hands to catch the kids' attention. They all immediately went back to the mats to take their positions. Betty led them to one of the bleachers, and they sat down.

Darcey watched, unable to take her eyes off him. All the students deferred to him, listening to every word he said.

"Sensei Stevens is one of our longest-serving volunteers," Betty explained. "Actually, before he was a volunteer, he used to come here all the time to take karate."

"He did?"

Betty nodded. "He was one of Sensei Toyama's best students. Eventually took over the class when Toyama decided he wanted to retire and go back to Okinawa six years ago. Sensei Stevens teaches three times a week when his schedule permits and hires a substitute paid out of his own pocket when he works days. He also comes in the mornings to bring us supplies and donations or do odd jobs after class before he heads off to work."

Was she hearing things? Anders took time out of his week to come here and volunteer? It was just so ... so not him. Everyone had told her about Anders's reputation, and not one of them had good things to say. Selfish. Uncouth. *Prick,* even. But not *this.*

Turning back to the class, she watched as he had them practicing kicks and punches in pairs. He ran a tight ship, and all of his students were focused on their tasks, though he would stop every once in a while to help someone who was having trouble or to give them tips.

Did she step into some kind of alternate dimension? Maybe this wasn't Anders but his twin, except that instead of being evil, this was his altruistic twin. Or a body-snatching alien.

As class wound down, everyone went back to their positions. Anders crossed his arms over his chest and scanned his gaze over them. He shouted something—Japanese, it sounded like—and everyone knelt down on the mats and closed their eyes.

He approached Janine and tapped her on the shoulder, then knelt down in front of the class.

"*Dojo-kun*," Janine shouted in what she probably thought was a fierce voice, but ended up sounding adorable. "Seek perfection of character." Her lisp made her sound even cuter.

"Seek perfection of character," everyone repeated.

"Be faithful," Janine added.

"Be faithful."

"Respect others."

"Respect others."

There was a pause. Janine opened her eyes and looked to Anders, who had cracked one eye open. As he fought the smile on his face, he mouthed something to her.

Janine nodded, closed her eyes again, and cleared her throat. "Refrain from violent behavior."

"Refrain from violent behavior."

Anders said something in Japanese, and the kids bowed. He bowed to them, and they all bowed together before standing up, then did a final bow before he said, "Class dismissed."

"Thank you, Sensei!" came the delighted chorus of the children, then they scattered about.

Anders picked up his water bottle from the corner, took a swig and grabbed his bag, then made his way over to them.

"Great class as always," Betty said. "Mary and her staff should have the snacks out. I'm sure your students are hungry after all that exercise."

Darcey cleared her throat. "This was really a great tour, Betty," she began. "Um, maybe we'll give you a call and let you know—"

"We're not going yet, are we, Darce?" Adam asked. "Betty hasn't even told us where they need volunteers, and I need this on my application. Can't we stay? It's not like you have anywhere to go."

Anders raised a brow, but she ignored him. "Right. I suppose we can stay and chat."

"Excellent," Betty said. "Let's go to the lunchroom."

They followed Betty out of the gym, the kids hurriedly jostling around them as they streamed out into the hallway. When they entered the lunchroom, food was already laid out on the tables, and each place setting had a tray with healthy drinks and snacks. Betty motioned for them to join her at the corner table with the other staff as the children excitedly took their places.

With everyone already seated and Adam needing to roll in at the head of the table, Darcey had no choice but to sit next to Anders, gingerly sliding along the bench, trying to seat herself as far away from him as possible without totally falling off the edge.

As they ate the snacks, Betty and the rest of the staff chatted and joked, asking Adam and her questions and telling them more about the community center, but Anders remained silent as a stone next to her.

"I didn't know you'd be here," she whispered to him, unable to bear the awkwardness between them. "I won't come here if you don't want me to."

"Good," he said gruffly, then bit into his sandwich. "I'd prefer it."

Her shoulders slumped. *Well, there was the Anders everyone knew and loved.* She knew he had to be lurking in there somewhere. Grabbing her juice, she tore the top open and shoved a straw in, then took a sip.

"So, Adam," Mary, the lady in charge of the kitchen began. "Are you here to take Sensei Steven's class too?"

"Oh no, this young man's here to offer his help. He says he's good at computers, maybe he can finally fix our printer." Betty grinned. "But, that's a good idea too. Anyone is free to join the class."

"I don't think so," Adam said bitterly.

"Why not?" Anders asked.

"Why not?" Her brother's eyes narrowed. "Are you stupid or something?" He glanced down at his lap.

"You poor thing. Was it an accident, dear?" Betty asked sympathetically. "Or were you born like that?"

Darcey gripped the edge of the table. *Oh no.* The only thing Adam hated more than talking about his disability was the pity and condescension from people who'd just met him. She knew it wasn't Betty's fault; she was trying to be nice, as were most people. They just didn't understand. *Adam, please,* she prayed silently. *Not here.*

Adam's lips pulled back into a thin line. "My dad beat the shit out of me when I was a kid, and I've been in a wheelchair ever since. Then my mom couldn't stand taking care of a cripple and so she left me in the care of the state."

"Adam!" she berated. Betty and Mary shifted in their seats uncomfortably, their faces red. "I'm sorry. He's not usually rude like this."

He sent her a glare. "I'm not the one being rude. Why do I have to shut up so people don't feel offended when I say the truth?"

Anders snorted. "Maybe you just can't hack my class, kid."

"Kid?" Adam bit out, then slapped his legs. "How the hell am I supposed to do all those moves with these?"

Anders took a deep breath, stood up and stepped out of the bench. Looking over the lunchroom, he caught someone's eye and then waved them over. A teen boy about Adam's age came forward to Adam, stopping two feet away. He wore the same white uniform as everyone else, though he had a brown belt around his waist. To Darcey's surprise, Anders made a motion with his hands, and the boy gestured back. *Sign language*, she recognized.

The teen bowed. Anders bowed back, then immediately reached out to strike the kid. Without flinching, he blocked Anders's hand, then the other, before grabbing them and twisting around, putting Anders in a lock with both arms behind him. With a quick tap, the boy released it, then the two faced each other and bowed. A smile spread across Anders's handsome face, and he signed something to the boy before he left to go back to his friends.

Turning to Adam, he said, "Well?"

Adam merely huffed. "It's not the same, though, is it?"

"Don't be a dumbass," Anders said.

Darcey looked at him incredulously, about to tear him a new one for calling her brother a dumbass, but he kept talking.

"What, you think Hector's got it easier than you? That he somehow lives in a different world that doesn't treat him less than someone who's 'normal'? Let me tell you something, kid, if you couldn't tell yet, life is hard. The world's going to kick your ass, whether you're small and defenseless or big and capable. Best you can do is learn to kick back. Now, apologize to these ladies for your language and ruining their meal with your shitty attitude." He turned to Betty. "Sorry about my language, ladies. I should go clean up the gym." Without another word, he spun on his heels and walked out of the lunchroom.

She just stared after him, not knowing what to say. Adam, on the other hand, muttered a "sorry" to the rest of the table.

"Apology accepted, Adam," Betty assured him. "And I apologize as well if I came off as condescending. It won't happen again."

The tension dissipated, and the rest of the meal passed by quickly. Darcey enjoyed chatting with the staff, which was why she felt sad at the thought that she couldn't volunteer, not when

Anders didn't want her here. He was here first, and they needed him more than her, so she would have to respect that. Adam could still come if he wanted to, but she would stay away.

After helping with cleanup, she headed out into the reception while Adam went to use the bathroom. She was about to take a seat when she heard a commotion outside. *What was that?*

Bounding out the door, she stopped at the threshold as the disturbance grew louder. It wasn't just any kind of ruckus, though. The harsh, heated words and cries were familiar enough to someone who'd grown up the way she did.

"I said, get in the car, Michelle!" The shabbily-dressed man bellowed. Tucked underneath his arm was a small figure with a mop of curly hair.

Janine!

The woman in front of him tried to make a grab for the girl, but the man pushed her away. "Ted, please!" she cried. "Don't hurt her."

"If you didn't want me to hurt her, then you shouldn't have run away," he scolded. "Now why would you do that? Did you think I wouldn't find you? Do you want to make me mad? Why do you make me like this?" He turned to the beat-up pickup truck behind him and opened the door.

Fury rose inside Darcey. And when Janine let out a pained wail as she was shoved inside the truck, something snapped inside her. Her swan blew out a hoarse whistle, raising its wings high. "Let her go!"

Ted pivoted, his bloodshot eyes training on her. "This is none of your business, bitch!"

An inhuman squawk ripped from her throat. A tingle rippled across her skin as her feathers pushed out of her arms.

"W-what the hell?" Ted's eyes widened.

Her clothes fell around her as her body shrank into her

74

swan form. Pushing her shirt out of the way, the swan raised its long neck and let out a long hiss directed at the foul man.

"Y-y-you're a—"

The swan lunged, wings snapping forward as it hit the man. *One. Two.* And again. *Thwack! Thwack!*

"What the—ow! Ow!" he cried as the swan's beak opened up and bit his nose, drawing blood. "God Almighty!" He swung his arms, but the swan was too fast and too strong. "Get it off me!" His body slammed on the ground with a thud as the swan continued its attack.

Darcey raged inside her swan, urging it to keep going. However, it let out an indignant shriek as something caught it from behind and pulled it away.

"Shh ... shh ... come on now, beautiful," a familiar, soothing voice cooed. "Calm down, Darcey. That's it."

Ooooh. The warm hands on her swan's body made Darcey go limp, as did her animal. It trilled excitedly and lay its head on a broad, muscled chest.

Oh no.

Of course it had to be *him.*

"There you go, beautiful." Anders smoothed a hand down the swan's wing, making it shake its head smugly. "Calm down now. It's fine. She's fine. Here."

The swan found itself deposited promptly on someone's lap —Adam's. Her brother held her gently, and she watched as Anders stalked toward the truck and the man who lay in a heap on the ground, bloody and wounded.

"Bastard," he spat as he stepped over the man and reached inside the truck, carefully taking out a tearful Janine. "You okay, sweetheart? That's right, don't worry. You'll be fine."

He handed the girl over to her waiting mother, who embraced her as the woman sobbed. He spoke softly to her and she nodded and thanked him. Then, he walked back over to them, picking up her discarded clothes before taking her from Adam again. "Betty's already called the police. I have the bastard's keys, but I don't think he's going anywhere." He shook his head. "You sure did do a number on him, beautiful. C'mon, let me take you to the bathroom so you can clean up."

He brought her inside the community center and headed to the female bathrooms. He placed her in the stall in the end, which was actually a shower, and hung her clothes on the hook. "I'll be waiting outside when you're ready," he said before shutting the stall door.

Ready? Oh God, was there a window here so she could escape? She didn't think she'd ever be ready to face him. Not after *that*.

Her swan, however, was practically glowing with happiness. Preening, really. Beautiful. Their mate called them *beautiful*. To be honest, she'd never been called that before. She was, after all, unusual, to say the least.

Slowly, her swan relinquished its hold on their body. Her feathers retracted back into her body, wings thinning back into arms. Soon, she stood naked in the shower stall. With a deep, calming sigh, she began to dress. But not in a hurry. Maybe if she took long enough, Anders would lose his patience and leave. Pushing the door open, she tiptoed out.

"Darcey?"

Dammit. No such luck. "Uh, hey," she said with a gulp.

Anders stared at her with an awestruck expression on him face. "So, you're a—"

"Swan," she finished.

"A *black* swan."

"Yes." She closed her eyes, thinking back to the day she shifted in her adult form for the first time. Her cygnet form looked like any other swan's—gray downy feathers with a black beak. Then one day, sometime around her eighteenth birthday, she had an uncontrollable shift when a boyfriend grabbed her by the wrist during an argument. Much to her surprise, instead of white feathers and an orange beak, she was black with a red beak.

"How are you feeling?"

That question unhinged her, and she burst into tears. As she covered her face with her hands, a pair of strong arms wrapped around her. *Oh.*

"Shh ... beautiful ..."

His embrace tightened, and she pressed her cheek against his chest, inhaling his maddeningly delicious scent. She knew she shouldn't do this. Knew that she should step away. But he just smelled and felt so *good.*

"What happened back there, Darcey?" he asked as he rubbed a hand down her back, the move sending a delicious thrill up her spine. "You know you can't just shift like that. In Blackstone it would be fine, but out here—"

"I know," she said. "I couldn't help it. I just ... I get triggered when I'm nervous or angry or I see ... I see someone getting hurt." Seeing that bastard shove Janine around like a rag doll brought back painful memories she didn't dare say aloud.

He stiffened. "Can't you control it? Did no one teach you? What about your parents?"

She sniffled. "I was adopted. Dropped off at an orphanage when I was a few days old. Wednesday isn't my real last name. I mean, it's my legal last name, but the nuns at St. Margaret gave it to me because that's the day they found me on their doorstep."

"And when you first shifted, you never practiced?"

"No. I rarely shifted into my swan. The nuns had been careful to conceal what I was. They thought if anyone found out I was a shifter, no one would adopt me." She let out a bitter laugh. "Not that it ever happened anyway. Don't get me wrong though, the nuns were kind to me. But I turned nine, and they couldn't let me stay. I went into the system, into different foster homes. I had to work harder to conceal my real nature. And then ..." She hiccupped. "I met Adam in one of those homes, and Sarah came a few months later. We made our own family."

"I did wonder," he said. "I didn't know Sarah was your sister, with her being human. But what about your real family?"

"Sarah and Adam *are* my real family," she said defensively. When she tried to pry herself away from him, he tightened his hold.

"Hey now. All right. I'm sorry for implying they aren't. And I'm sorry about your parents abandoning you."

"That's one way to think about it."

"One way?"

Looking up at him, she could see the flummoxed expression on his face. "I mean, yeah, I could think that they abandoned me. Th-that they didn't want me. Or maybe they had to give me up for a good reason."

His jaw hardened. "What good reason would a mother have for abandoning a cub?"

"I dunno. There could be a lot. Maybe she was young and couldn't provide for me. Maybe she loved me enough to give me up."

He snorted. And honestly, that made her smile. Because it was so ... Anders.

"Um, I'm sorry I ruined your shirt." She blushed, looking at the tracks of tears on the white fabric.

"Meh, it's fine." His arms dropped to his sides. "You ready? I think Adam nearly fainted when he saw you open a can of whoop-ass on that dickhead." He grinned. "Remind me never to piss you off, by the way."

"Ha! You better not."

She followed him out of the bathroom to the reception area where Adam waited for them, along with the other volunteers.

There was also a police officer in uniform there, interviewing them. Darcey stopped, her heart thudding loudly in her chest. *Oh no.*

"... Yes, Officer Nealy," Betty said in her sweetest voice. "When Mr. Howard came here to try and take Janine, a big bird came from nowhere and started attacking him."

Nealy raised a brow. "A bird?"

"Uh-huh. Cross my heart, officer." As she did the sign, her gaze caught Darcey's and she winked.

"I think it's that time of the year," Mary added. "When the geese from Canada pass by during their migration. You know how vicious those birds can be."

Nealy huffed. "Right." He asked them a few more questions before he was satisfied. "Thanks for your cooperation, ladies, I'll be in touch." With a tip of his hat, he headed out toward the exit and left.

Darcey looked at the two older women gratefully. "Thank you."

"No, thank you, Darcey," Betty said. "You did good, child."

"We should get going, it's getting late," she said. "Adam?"

"Yeah, yeah. Thanks, Miss Betty, Miss Mary," he said. "We'll see you soon."

"Bye now," Betty greeted.

"Drive safe," Mary added.

"I'll walk you to your car," Anders said.

"You don't—"

"C'mon, Darce," Adam huffed. "We don't have all day."

"All right, all right." She bit her lip. "Let's go."

They headed out to the parking lot, toward the accessible van that they had borrowed from Daniel's parents. Taking the key fob out of her purse, she opened the door. As Adam slid into the back seat, she turned to Anders. "Don't worry, I won't be volunteering here," she began.

"It's fi—"

"No." She held up a hand. "It's too dangerous for me." It was technically the truth, but she didn't dare elaborate on why. "Adam might want to come back, and Sarah or I will drop him off and pick him up. But otherwise, you don't have to worry."

"Darcey—"

"No, it's fine. I'll find something else. There's a senior center on the other side of town, maybe I can do something there."

He muttered something under his breath.

What was the matter *now*? "Excuse me?"

"I said," he took a deep breath. "Don't come on Tuesdays."

"Tuesdays?"

"It's bingo night," he said. "And I'm the host."

It was a wonder her jaw didn't literally dislodge from her skull and drop to the floor. Who the heck was this man? "Fine. No Tuesday night volunteering." She blew out an exasperated breath. Was there anything else she needed to know about his secret life? Did he save puppies from burning buildings? Help blind people across the street? Rescue kittens from trees? "Goodbye, Anders."

"Bye, Darcey."

She slipped into the driver's seat and started the engine. "You okay back there?" she asked, looking up at the rearview mirror to meet Adam's gaze.

He gave her a thumbs-up. "Yup, all strapped in."

Putting the van in reverse, she pulled out of the handicap parking spot. Much to her surprise, Anders hadn't moved at all, but continued to stare at the van. Right at where she was sitting. Her cheeks warmed, thinking of that oddly intimate scene in the bathroom.

"You know," Adam began as she maneuvered the van out of the lot. "I kinda like him."

She slammed on the brakes. "You what?"

"Whoa there!" Adam chuckled as he steadied himself. "And yeah, I do. He reminds me of Daniel."

"Excuse me?" Was Adam insane? "He's nothing like Daniel. Daniel is polite and nice. The perfect gentleman. Anders is rude and—"

"No, not like *that*." Adam rolled his eyes. "Anders ... he doesn't treat me different; you know? Like I'm made of glass or a porcelain egg or some shit. He's not afraid to tell me I'm being a dumbass when I'm acting like one, just because I'm in a wheelchair."

Her brother's words made her pause. Had it really never occurred to her or Sarah that maybe Adam wanted to be treated like any other kid? Because of his disability, they'd coddled and hovered over him. She swallowed hard. They hadn't been doing him any favors, treating him like he could break at any moment. The truth was, Adam was a lot stronger than they thought.

"So, do *you* like him?"

"What?" She whirled her head back to face him. "No, I don't."

Adam raised his chin at her smugly. "Uh-huh."

She rolled her eyes. "Let's go home." Facing back to the wheel, she put the van in gear and pulled out onto the road. As they drew farther away, her swan sighed sadly.

God, was she always going to feel this way, drawn to him, pining for him? Daniel's words from this morning came back to her thoughts. She just had to make sure they never bonded. But staying away might not be enough.

Later that evening, as she lay in bed not feeling tired at all, she reached for her phone on her bedside. The missed calls from Cam made guilt seep through her, and so she called him back.

"Darcey," he greeted.

"Cam." Not even his gorgeous accent made her feel

anything. But she pushed on. "Um, I saw your missed calls. Sorry, did you want to check on me after the break-in?"

"Break-in? What break-in?"

He didn't even know. Or care. "Never mind. Why did you call?"

"Ah, yes." He cleared his throat. "I was wondering, there's an event this weekend that Damon wants us all to attend. Fancy charity event. Black tie, that kind of thing. Would you be my date?"

"Oh." She tried to muster up all the enthusiasm she had. And utterly failed. "Sure."

"Excellent. I'll send you the invite in the morning. Goodnight."

"Goodnight, Cam." She plopped back on her pillows. This was it. Her third date with Cam. Daniel said that his biological parents had a happy life even though they weren't mates. Maybe this was the only way she could truly stop yearning for Anders.

Chapter 6

The night shift stretched on and on with nothing to occupy Anders and his tiger except the silence of the evening, broken only by the various sounds of the forest around him and his own thoughts. Thoughts which inevitably led to one thing, or rather, one person.

Darcey Wednesday.

He didn't expect to see her at the community center. Hell, he didn't expect to see her at all. Though seeing her hurt that night had his tiger's protective instincts flaring, he pushed it deep down. He'd already vowed to stay away and forget about her.

Then she just walked right in to the one place he never wanted anyone to see him. The community center was the only place he felt safe enough to let anyone close, as much as he could allow it. Growing up, it had been his sanctuary from the stuff going on at home.

If it wasn't for the community center, and Betty and Mary and Sensei Toyama, his life would have taken a different path. He owed the center a lot, which was why he gave back as much as he could. Every day he was there, he saw himself in those kids, but the only way to reach them was to open himself up, even just a little.

Seeing Darcey there made him feel exposed and raw. Made him feel things he didn't want to feel. Not to mention, seeing her shifter side ... well, that didn't help at all.

She was beautiful—no, magnificent—and so was her swan. *A black swan.* He could hardly believe it even when he did see it. What was that they said about black swans? Supposedly, they were used to describe a rare, unpredictable event.

That's what Darcey was. An unpredictable event in his life.

Only, he already knew what would happen. Could predict it. But he would fight it before he ruined her.

His thoughts continued to spiral. If only she hadn't come to Blackstone. If only Daniel hadn't married Sarah during that night of debauchery. The irony wasn't lost on him, however, because *he* was the one who forced the bachelor party in Vegas. All because he didn't want to be alone with his thoughts and memories on his birthday. Pride and keeping his carefully cultivated reputation made it difficult to tell the guys the real reason he wanted to go to Vegas—that he wanted to be surrounded by the people he considered friends, even though they might not feel the same way about him.

Finally, he was at the end of his shift, and he caught a ride with transport back to HQ. As he sat in the back of the truck, he reached into his pocket and removed something that he'd been itching to touch. Opening his palms, he stared down at it. The object he shouldn't have kept, but couldn't bear to throw away.

A single black feather.

It wasn't overly big, maybe four or five inches long, curled at the edges and a pure midnight in color. Lifting it to his nose, he could smell traces of Darcey's sweet, intoxicating scent.

The truck jolted to a stop, and he tucked the feather away into his front shirt pocket before anyone saw it. Thanking the driver, he hopped out and headed into HQ. After a quick shower and changing into his street clothes, he headed out. He was about to grab the door when it opened, and Damon stepped in.

"Chief," he greeted.

"Anders," Damon replied. "Just the man I wanted to see."

"Me?" he asked. "What's up, chief?"

Damon motioned for them to step aside, and Anders followed him. "Just wanted to remind you about the Blackstone Rangers Anniversary Ball this weekend."

Fuck me. "Yeah and so?"

Damon scratched his chin. "It's come to my attention that you've missed every single one of them since you joined."

He snorted. "Yeah, those things really ain't my style."

"This year it will be."

"Are you *fucking* kidding me?"

One of Damon's dark brows shot up, and he rose up to full height, hands on his hips. "Wanna try that again?"

Anders gnashed his teeth together. "All these years, Simpson didn't care if I went or not," he said, mentioning the previous chief of the Blackstone rangers before Damon. "Why should you?"

"Because you know attendance is mandatory," Damon pointed out. "It's an official function, and the Lennoxes will want every one of us there for support. Our biggest donors will be there."

His blood froze in his veins. That was *exactly* why he didn't want to go. "You don't need me there. I'll swap shifts with anyone who wants to attend your fancy party."

Damon crossed his arms over his chest. "You're going."

"No."

"If Krieger can make it, so can you."

"What?" John Krieger was coming to a fancy dress party? It

almost made him want to go. Almost. "That doesn't mean shit. So, let him get dressed up like a trained monkey. What's it to you, anyway?"

"I don't want to be accused of favoritism; you know I need to treat everyone equally. Look, just come this once, and I won't get on your case about it for another couple of years."

"Why are you hell-bent on having me there?" He eyed Damon suspiciously. Of course, the chief's expression betrayed nothing. "Are you going to drag me out there if I decide not to go?"

"I could. Or I could make things harder for you to get the shifts you want."

Motherfucker. "Fine," he relented.

"Great." Damon took something out of his pocket. "Here's the invite. Don't forget to RSVP with your plus-one."

"Plus—hey, hold on a minute—"

"I'm late to a meeting," Damon said, brushing him aside. "See you around."

"You never said anything about a plus-one!" *Shit. Shit, shit, shit.* But Damon was already gone. Otherwise, he would have told the chief to suck it.

With an angry growl, he stuffed the invitation in his pocket and stalked to his pickup. Getting inside, he lay his forehead on the wheel and let out an annoyed grunt.

Fuck Damon, fuck that anniversary ball, and fuck his life. He supposed it wasn't all that terrible. And there would probably be hundreds of people at the ball. All of Blackstone's elite, dressed to the nines. Anxiety edged into his chest, and his heart pounded, but he pushed it aside.

What were the chances he'd run into *them? Slim,* he told himself. He'd get dressed, parade around in front of Damon, and get the fuck out of there.

Of course, that only solved one problem. He still needed a date.

Shit. He hadn't been on a date in years. And frankly, it had been a while since he'd even been with any woman. No, his playboy, skirt-chasing act was, well, just that. An *act.* The last time was ... well, he didn't want to *think* how long it had been. It wasn't that he didn't like sex, but it was too risky and left him feeling too vulnerable.

So, he didn't even have anyone in his contacts that he could call up to be his date, and he didn't have a lot of woman friends, except for the ladies at the community center. Maybe he could ask around if any of the female rangers already had dates, but he doubted any of them would go with him considering his reputation.

An idea popped into his head. There was *one* female he could think of to ask.

Revving up the engine, he started the long drive down the mountain. When he got to the road at the bottom, he turned east instead of west, and made his way to Blackstone town proper, just a few blocks off Main Street, and pulled into a compound that took up most of the block, driving under a sign that proclaimed it as J.D.'s Garage.

After parking his truck next to the small office trailer, he headed toward the workshops, stopping one of the guys to ask where the boss was, who then directed him toward the middle of the three buildings onsite. When he got there, another employee pointed to the yellow Honda sitting in the end, where a figure clad in overalls was bent over the front.

"Hey, J.D.!" he called.

The sound of something hitting metal and a curse came from under the hood. "Shit-licking fuck-trumpets, you guys know never to sneak up on—oh." J.D. looked out from behind the hood, rubbing her head. As usual, her messy blonde hair was tucked under a trucker cap, and a spot of grease marred her cheek. "It's you." Her eyes narrowed at him, and he could swear he felt her animal hiss at him and extend its claws.

"Hey, kitty," he teased. "What's shaking?"

Her nostrils flared. Though J.D. had never shifted in front of him, nor had she confirmed what she was, Anders could tell she was definitely feline. "What do you want? I'm up to my ears in work, and I don't have time to deal with your shit too."

"I'll get to the point," he began. "You're a girl."

Rolling her eyes, she pulled the neckline of her overalls and peered down. "Yep. Tits're still there, so yeah, I'm a girl all right."

"There's this party this weekend at Blackstone Castle. And I need a date."

"So?"

"So maybe, you and I can go together."

"I'd rather shit in my hands and clap," she said, not missing a beat.

"Don't hold back, now, McNamara. Tell me how you *really* feel about me." He blew out a breath. "Why the hell not?"

"Why the hell would I?" she shot back. "A girl can't even breathe on you without being chalked up as another notch on your bedpost. Besides, I've already put on a fancy dress once this year at Damon's wedding, and that's about my limit."

"C'mon, J.D.," he said. "Do it as a favor? For me?"

"And why would I do that? What do you want me for? Don't you have a million girls in your phone? Go bother one of them." She waved him away.

"Do you know anyone else who would want to go with me? How about that friend of yours, the cute redhead who makes dresses?"

"Ha. As if Dutchy would even give you the time of day," she snorted. "Why are you desperate for a date, anyway?"

"Damon's making me go," he moaned. "I don't have a choice."

"So? Go alone," she said. "It's not like they're going to stop you from entering if you're by yourself. If it makes you feel better, tell them I was gonna go, but I got sick." Picking up a wrench, she waved it at him. "Now, will you please stop bothering me and leave? You won't find a date here." She cocked her head toward a group of mechanics at the other end. "Unless you're thinking of strolling into Blackstone Castle with Big George on your arm. I bet he'll look cute in a dress and heels."

He ground his teeth together. "Fine. I'll say my date cancelled last minute."

As he left the garage, his hand instinctively went to his pants pocket, stroking the feather he had transferred there from his uniform pocket. There was one person he really wanted to take to this ball; in fact, she was the first one he thought of when Damon said he needed a date.

"*Gahhh.*" He shook his head and took his hand out of his pocket. There was no way he was going to ask Darcey to come to that ball with him. He was already dreading the worst-case scenario of what could happen there. She didn't need that shit to touch her too. And in any case, going alone would make it easier to slip out once he was done.

———

By the night of the anniversary party, Anders was a ball of nervous anxiety. Breathing techniques that Sensei Toyama taught him had helped, but faced with the prospect of being in the same room as *them* was making his chest constrict and his heart pound. His tiger sensed his unease, and though it remained silent, he could feel the tension building in his animal.

One hour, tops, he told himself as he pulled up to the front of Blackstone Castle. Even as he handed his keys to the waiting valet, all he wanted to do was yank the keys back and drive in the opposite direction. Or shift into his tiger form and run into the mountains.

Get a grip.

Swallowing hard, he pulled at the collar of his tux, feeling suffocated and itchy. He didn't exactly have formal clothes lying around, so he had to rent this one. There wasn't much time to have it fitted, and it was still tight around the shoulders. He wouldn't be wearing it too long anyway, so it didn't matter.

"This way, sir," a severe-looking waiter gestured to the hallway on the left. "The ballroom is at the end."

"Thanks, bud," he said, patting the man on the shoulder.

As he made his way to the ballroom, he already felt out of place just walking down the richly-decorated hallway filled with expensive artwork and plush furniture. He'd never even stepped foot in this house before, the home of the Blackstone Dragons. Though he'd been in school around the same time as Jason and Matthew Lennox, he wasn't exactly part of their elite circle; not when he was the boy from the wrong side of town, growing up in a trailer that was probably smaller than the castle's foyer.

Music swelled as he entered the ballroom. Just as he'd predicted, it was packed, which made some of the tension in his body leave. Maybe it wasn't going to be so bad. He could survive this night without having it turn into a complete disaster.

You can do this, he told himself as he pushed into the crowd. A passing waiter offered a glass of champagne from the tray he carried, but Anders waved him away. He was going to be okay.

Of course, all positive thoughts evaporated the moment he felt his tiger's ear perk up at the sound of a familiar voice.

"... and did you manage to find that species of antelope?"

"Of course," came the reply in that snooty accent that grated his ears.

His back stiffened, and despite his mind screaming at him to walk away, he turned around instead. Sure enough, it was Darcey, looking devastatingly beautiful in a long black gown that hugged her figure and showed off her creamy skin, her long locks of white-blonde hair in waves down her shoulders. Her arm was looped around Dr. Cam Spenser, staring up at him. The smile on her face made his gut clench and a hot, tight feeling seeped into his chest.

She must have sensed his gaze because she turned his head. Her face had the proverbial deer in headlights look when their eyes met. "A-Anders," she stammered. "What are you doing here?"

He clenched and unclenched his jaw. "This is an official Blackstone Rangers event. Why wouldn't I be here?" He turned to Cam. "Didn't think you'd take time away from peeping into birds' nests and bagging shit samples to grace us with your presence."

"Certain dung specimens can be more interesting than *some* people," Cam said coolly, the corner of his lips lifting up to a barely imperceptible smile. "But the company of a beautiful woman always trumps everything else." His arm snaked around Darcey's waist, the fingers gripping her just below her breast.

Hot jealousy stabbed in his chest like a knife. His tiger was ready to lunge at this male for daring to touch her, but he managed to pull it back. God, he really wished he'd gotten some champagne from that waiter. "Well, I'll be seeing you around."

"Anders—"

Not bothering to let her finish, he turned on his heel and walked away. Casually, at first, but when he was sure he was lost in the crowd, his pace picked up and he glanced around anxiously. His throat felt dry, and so he headed toward the bar in the far corner of the ballroom, clumsily pushing people aside who didn't move out of his way fast enough.

The line for the bar was two-deep, but he didn't care. He wedged himself between two women and made a grab for the man who was leaning against the bar.

"Hey, what the hell is the matter with you?"

He spun the other man around to face him. "I need a—"

Fuck, no.

It was hard to describe the feeling that slammed into his brain. Like a complete one-eighty, from the jealousy over Cam holding Darcey and now *this*.

Unsettling.

Unnerving.

Shocking.

Bile rose in his throat as he stared into golden eyes.

"I said, what the hell's the matter with you?"

The man was probably a decade younger than Anders, and that arrogant smirk on his face made him look even more youthful. From the way his tux was cut perfectly to his body to the expensive watch on his wrist, it was obvious he was wealthy. Certainly rich enough to be invited here.

He was also a shifter, but Anders didn't need to reach out and try to feel his animal. It would only confirm what he already knew. Confirm who this kid was.

"Christopher, darling," a refined feminine voice said from behind. "Did you get me that drink?"

"I was going to, Mother. Until this man cut the line," he sneered.

"Excuse—"

Anders turned around, folding his hands over his chest.

"Me?" The woman turned a deathly pale white as every drop of blood drained from her face.

The fear in her eyes was almost satisfying. Almost. "Hello, Felicia."

"Mother?" Christopher moved protectively in front of her. "Who is this man?"

Felicia swallowed, then turned to him. "Nobody, darling," she said nervously. "No one you need to know." Looping her arm through his, she tugged at him. "Actually, you know what, I've had enough to drink for tonight. Why don't we go back to your father's table and sit down for a moment? He's been dying to introduce you to Hank Lennox." Without another glance at Anders, she led him away.

As he stared after them, Anders didn't dare move. Not when his chest was ready to collapse into itself, and the only thing preventing it from crushing his lungs was pure willpower.

"Anders?"

Christ. "Not now, Darcey," he whispered in a hoarse voice. Oh God, please. Not now.

A hand came up to touch his arm, feathery soft. "Are you all right?" she asked. "You look like you've seen a ghost."

He did, in a way. Shutting his eyes, he didn't dare look at her. Yet, her scent, her presence, was all around him. Like the entire ballroom filled with people had melted away and it was just him and Darcey there.

"Who was that? He looks like—"

With a growl, he pushed past her and stalked into the sea of people, wishing they would swallow him whole like the real ocean so he didn't have to feel this way anymore.

Chapter 7

Try as she might, Darcey couldn't stay away from Anders. For one thing, her swan had been annoyed the entire evening. It hated Cam's touch and smell and everything about him. Then when they bumped into Anders, it got even worse. She could feel it pushing against her skin, wanting to break free. So, when Anders strode off, she made some excuse to Cam and went after him.

He had been talking to a young man and an older woman, but the din around her prevented her from focusing on their conversation.

But, why did it feel like she knew them, or at least, had seen them before? Whoever, they were, they had upset Anders, though upset was a mild world to describe the look on his face.

Darcey knew heartbreak well, and if her instincts were correct, she had just witnessed it.

Mine! Her swan beat its wings insistently, but it didn't have to urge her on. No, something else inside her propelled her forward to chase after Anders.

"Wait!" she called. Her eyes never lost track of him, even in the growing crowd of fancy ballgowns and black tuxes. It was as if she could pinpoint exactly where he was, like some kind of homing device. He was fast, but she could keep up, and there was only one exit out of the ballroom.

He turned and she followed him, down a long corridor. Then the next corner. And then the next. *How big was this place?* It was huge from the outside, but in here, it was cavernous. Finally, the footsteps stopped, and Anders was nowhere in sight.

Where did he go?

Closing her eyes, she focused her hearing. *There.* Shuffling behind one of the doors. Moving closer, she reached for the handle, turning it and peeking inside. Sure enough, she saw Anders, his back to her as he leaned over the sink, palms planted at the edge of the marble. Quietly, she walked inside, closing the door gently behind her and locking it.

His head whipped up, their gazes meeting in the reflection of the mirror, his eyes like twin fires. "I said, not now, Darcey."

Pain rolled off him, and she couldn't help herself. Her swan flapped its wings, distressed at his condition. Seeing him like this, in agony ... she couldn't stop herself from coming closer to him, no more than she could stop the waves from crashing on the shore or the sun from setting every night. "What's wrong? Tell me?" She raised a hand up, her fingers centimeters away from his face when she found herself pushed backward, her body caged against the door as Anders held her tight against it.

"You want to know what's wrong?" he said savagely, his eyes burning like molten gold. "Let me tell you a story."

"Anders, I—" She flinched when his fingers dug into her skin.

"Listen up, buttercup, it's a good one. A love story. Girls like you eat this shit up, or so I heard." He gnashed his teeth. "Once upon a time, there was a beautiful tigress. One day, she met her mate—her fated mate. A lynx shifter who was as handsome as

Lucifer and rich as sin. Their eyes met across a busy street, and she knew he was the one fate had intended for her. And so, they lived happily ever after, their mate bond ensuring that they would never, ever be apart." Contempt dripped from his every word, and he continued. "Except it wasn't as simple as happy ever after. The tigress was already married, see. To a human who didn't understand things like bonding and fate and mates. She also had a son with him.

"But the urge to be with her mate was stronger, stronger than anything else in the world. Stronger than her love for her human husband and her cub. Her old family was in the way, ruining her happy ever after. So, what could she do but leave them behind, pretend they never existed, so she could live with her mate and start her new family. Her rightful family fate had chosen. The day she walked out, she didn't even remember that it was the cub's birthday."

Realization swept through her as a pit grew in her stomach. Who that man and woman were, who had the same eyes as Anders.

She bit the inside of her cheek to keep from crying out. "W-what happened to her cub?" Dread filled her, but she needed to know. To understand.

"What do you think? Left behind with a father who didn't know how to raise him, who only knew the bottom of a bottle of booze each night." He closed his eyes, pain marring his handsome face. "He blamed his shifter wife for leaving him. Most of all, he blamed the cub, couldn't stand to look at him as he reminded him of why his wife left him. It was the cub's fault, and he let him know every single day with the back of his fist. That he deserved the brunt—"

"No!" She couldn't stand seeing him like this, agony eating him up. "It wasn't your fault!" Reaching up, she cupped his face in her hands. "It's not. Your. Fault." Was it any wonder that

Anders thought that the idea of her mother having good reasons to leave her at an orphanage absurd? Swallowing the lump in her throat, she stared into his eyes. The emptiness in them made her heart crack. "You were a child. They were the adults. They could have worked something out."

"Nobody," he spat. "That's what she called me tonight. In front of *him*. Looked at me like she never even knew me."

A deep anger began to boil inside her. "Well, that makes her an asshole. She didn't have to cut you out of her life completely. You didn't deserve that."

"Maybe I did. Maybe I was a bad—"

She didn't know how to stop him from talking, so she launched herself at him, pushing him back until his back hit the sink. "No!" she cried, digging her fingers into his arms. "Don't say that! You weren't a bad kid and you're not a bad person now. You're wonderful and kind and selfless."

He lowered his head, and the emptiness in his eyes began to fill with something else. Something blazing hot. Time slowed down, and it was as if a string was pulling at her, bringing her closer to him. Not just physically, but something else she couldn't describe.

And in a desperate moment, their lips met.

Fire blazed inside her, consuming her. And God help her, she wanted to burn. His lips devoured her, like he, too, was being eaten alive with desire from the inside. Her fingers slid up to his scalp, raking her nails into his hair until he moaned into her mouth.

His hands reached behind her, unzipping her dress so he could yank down the front. She whimpered when his mouth left hers to trail a hot path down her neck, then lower to her bared chest. He didn't waste time as he nibbled and sucked at her breasts, drawing as much as he could of the flesh into his mouth while his free hand cupped and played with her other nipple.

She cried out as his teeth grazed at her, pain melding with pleasure. He bent down, his hands pushing up the skirt of her dress to her waist, then hoisted her on top of the marble counter.

"Anders!" She moaned as he knelt in front of her, then made quick work of her panties. "You can't—" Her lips clamped shut and her eyes rolled back into her head when his mouth touched her already slick pussy.

The wet, filthy sounds of his lips licking and feasting on her echoed in the small bathroom. His strong hands kept her thighs spread open, holding her in place even as she squirmed under his mouth. His lips and—oh God—his tongue, devoured and gorged on her like he hadn't eaten in days. He licked at her, teasing at her lips and then her clit, sucking back on the bud until she was shuddering with pleasure.

She barely had time to come down from her orgasm when he stood up, towering over her even with her sitting on the counter. His eyes blazed with naked, raw desire as they searched hers, asking without saying anything.

Mesmerized by the hot fury of passion building inside her, she reached down to his pants. How she managed to unbuckle his belt while her fingers shook, she didn't know, but in seconds, she was unzipping him and reaching inside to take out his fully erect, naked cock.

Her hands encircled his shaft, stroking it. A breath caught in her throat as she felt him grow even heavier and larger, his excitement evident from his rough gasps. Moving herself forward, she guided his tip to her entrance.

"Darcey," he moaned and pushed inside her, spreading her, slowly filling her. "God," he whispered when he was fully inside her.

She closed her eyes as he gathered her to his chest, strong arms holding her, and she clung to him as he began to move. As his movements began to grow quicker, she managed to wrap her legs around him, urging him deeper.

He held her tighter, one hand snaking up to behind her neck possessively as he collared her throat, then captured her mouth again. His kissed her deep, licking and nipping at her as he let out a growl and continued his relentless thrusting, the pressure of her impending orgasm building like a tight, hot ball inside her.

She let out a yelp when he pulled out and she found herself whirled around; her waist pushed up against the counter. Anders caught one leg and hoisted it up, her knee resting on the cold marble. Moving up behind her, he lined up his cock and pushed fully into her.

She closed her eyes and slammed her palms against the mirror, bracing herself as he moved again, rutting into her, his grunts and moans triggering something primal inside her. His hands steadied her hips as he continued to pummel into her until she was shuddering with pleasure again.

"Open your eyes, beautiful," came the low growl, his breath hot in her ear. Slowly, she did open them and met his blazing molten gaze in the mirror. His expression was tense, but it only made him look more handsome, and if she were honest, a thrill of power came over her knowing that look of pleasure on his face was because of her.

"So ... good ... Darcey," he bit out. "Beautiful. Beautiful Darcey."

"Don't ... hold ... back," she breathed out. "I can take it." She winced when he thrust in particularly hard but met his gaze again. There was something there she couldn't name. Desire, yes, but also some deep longing he was holding back. "Do it."

He let out a snarl, then thrust his fingers into her hair. Savagely, he pounded into her, grabbing one of her arms and pinning it behind her. All the time, his gaze never left hers in the reflection of the mirror.

Wrapping her hair around a fist, he pulled her head back and clamped his mouth on her neck, sucking on her skin and flesh. His teeth bit into her, and the pleasure that tore through her body came from nowhere.

He let out a grunt, primal and deep and masculine as she felt his cock pulse inside her. She moaned, pushing her ass back to meet his erratic thrusts as his body shuddered with aftershocks and his arms encircled her torso, holding her tight.

He groaned as he pressed kisses on her neck and shoulders. As his grip around her loosened and his cock slipped out of her, she sank back against him, leaning against him for support. Her legs were shaking as she eased herself upright.

"Darcey," he breathed against her ear. "Let's get out of here."

Her head snapped back up to meet his eyes in the mirror. "Out ... of here?"

"This was just a taste, beautiful." He grazed his mouth over her neck, making her shiver. "I could go all night with you. Make you come over and over again until you beg me to stop." He took a step away from her, then fumbled at his waist to right himself.

She sucked in a breath into her deflating lungs, the oxygen somehow clearing her addled brain too. Her body, despite feeling exhausted from the orgasms he'd already wrung from her, wanted what he promised.

But something made her pause. The sex was phenomenal, and she knew he wasn't exaggerating. She would probably beg him, but then what? What happened after that? What would happen tomorrow? "I ... I can't."

"My truck's out—wait, what do you mean, you can't?"

The air grew thick around them, but she resisted the urge to appease him. *I'm a strong, independent woman*, she repeated to herself. "The party's still going on out there." Fumbling at her gown, she managed to hoist the top up over her breasts and then turned to face him.

"So?" he asked, his tone irritated. "Who gives a fuck about those rich bastards out there? What do they have to do with us?"

"Us?" She crossed her arms under her chest. "And what is 'us' exactly?"

His dark brows snapped together, then he opened his mouth, but shut it quickly.

Her heart sank, but she mentally shook her head. "Yeah, that's what I thought." God, she was an idiot. Why did she have sex with him? And in a bathroom of all places?

They had been caught up in the moment. And oh—his mother. That's who that woman was, right? That *bitch* was still out there. Outrage fueled inside her at how she'd treated Anders. At what he had gone through, having his mother abandon him and then pretend he never existed.

"Don't," he bit out.

"Don't?" She blinked. "What do you—"

"Don't look at me like that," he spat, his gaze hardening like steel. "Save your pity for someone else."

"I'm not—" She flinched when he growled and pinned her to the counter, his arms trapping her against the cool marble. "Anders."

He let out a brusque huff. "Stay here then. Go on. Drink champagne, and dance the night away in your precious Cam's arms. Maybe he can make you forget about how hard I made you come. Or how loud you screamed while I was deep inside you, fucking your brains out. I don't think that icicle is up to the task, but I'm sure he'd give it the good ol' college try."

The cruel words hit their mark, right in the heart. But she

refused to bleed for him. "Is it your goal to make everyone think you're a heartless bastard?"

"I'm not what you think I am. I'm not what you want me to be. So, last chance, Darcey," he taunted, stroking a finger up and down her arm. "What'll it be?"

"Get out," she hissed.

His expression inscrutable, he pushed himself off the counter, spun on his heels, and walked out.

When the door slammed shut, she expelled the breath she'd been holding onto for dear life. *How could I let this happen?* One moment she was could feel his anguish and pain over his mother's treatment and the next they were having sex in a bathroom. In a stranger's home.

Whirling around, she looked at her reflection in the mirror. Oh Lord, she was a mess. Her lipstick and hair were mussed, her dress was crooked. She had a hickey the size of Texas on her neck. And her damn panties ... well they were gone. *And my best pair, too, from Sarah's latest collection.*

She groaned. Sarah and Daniel were out there. And so was *Cam.* Her *date.* Had she forgotten about them? The urge to slip out of the castle undetected was strong, but Cam had picked her up, so she had no ride back home.

With a deep sigh, she turned on the faucet and splashed water on her face. Somehow, she had to make it back outside and pretend nothing happened.

———

"Darcey?" Sarah asked. "Are you okay?" She was seated at their table with the rest of their group which consisted of Damon, Anna Victoria, Gabriel, Temperance, Sarah, and Daniel. When she arrived with Cam earlier that evening, Anna Victoria had looked surprised, but guided them over to the table they had reserved.

There had been another man across the table, someone she didn't recognize, but he must have been a ranger too. He didn't say a word nor introduce himself, but it was hard to ignore him with his hulking size, long dark hair, and thick beard. Even though he was seated, he still towered over everyone. But that wasn't what caught her attention. It was the way he looked at her with his razor-sharp gaze. The glance was brief, but she shivered at those eyes boring into her. Her swan, too, had twittered nervously in his presence. He was gone now, and she couldn't help but feel relief that she didn't have to be around him.

"Me?" she said, as casually as she could possibly make it sound. "Yeah, I'm fine."

"You were gone an awful long time." Her sister eyed her suspiciously.

"You look a little flushed," Daniel added.

"Needed some air, then I got lost." She forced out a chuckle. "This place is huge!"

"There you are."

She stiffened, feeling Cam's presence behind her. His hand came to rest on the small of her back, and she peered up at him. "Yup, here I am. Were you looking for me?"

"I'm sure you were all right," he said.

Though she should have been miffed her date didn't even think to find her after she'd been gone for half an hour, she actually felt relief. After Anders had left, she did her best to clean up in the bathroom, covering her healing hickey with her hair and scrubbing away her smeared lipstick. Cam didn't seem to suspect anything, so she probably did a good job removing all traces of Anders on her.

Her swan pecked at her, annoyed.

Oh, shut it.

"Um, sorry I had to run off. I had a chat with this lady who wanted to visit the store. Did you have a good time mingling?" she asked.

"Actually, that's why I came to find you." Those icy violet blue eyes focused on her, making her stomach flutter with nervousness.

"Really? Why?"

"I met someone you might find interesting. Come, I'll introduce you to him. Will you excuse us?" he said to the rest of the group as he led her away.

They didn't go too far, only to the next group two tables over. Cam tapped the shoulder of a man with white hair who was sitting down, chatting with a woman next to him. "Excuse me, Dr. Marsh?"

The white-haired man stopped talking to his companion and craned his neck up. "Oh, Dr. Spenser, you're back."

"Yes, and I've brought that young woman I wanted to introduce you to."

"Of course, yes." Dr. Marsh stood up. He was tall, though slightly on the portly side. She guessed he was probably in his mid-fifties.

"Dr. Alfred Marsh," Cam began. "This is Darcey Wednesday."

"Nice to meet you." She offered her hand. But who was this man?

Dr. Marsh's kind face lit up into a smile. "I've been looking forward to meeting you, Miss Wednesday."

"Me?" She chuckled. "Why would—" As Dr. Marsh took her hand, the most peculiar sensation came over her. She always knew when she was meeting another shifter, especially back when she lived in Vegas, but this was an odd, familiar feeling. Like she knew him. *Really* knew him. "You—"

"That's right." Dr. Marsh nodded. "I'm a swan. Just like you."

She sucked in a breath and looked up at Cam, then back at Dr. Marsh. "Wow. I mean. Oh." Her swan fluttered around excitedly inside her. "I've never met another swan before," she said, flustered at her reaction. "Sorry, it's a bit overwhelming."

"No need to apologize, Miss Wednesday." He covered her hands with his reassuringly. "There are so very few bevies in the world. Tell me, which one do you belong to?"

"I don't belong to any," she said. "I was adopted. Left by my parents at an orphanage when I was a baby."

His eyes widened, and his mouth rounded into a perfect *O*. "But that ... I mean ..." He cleared his throat. "That seems ... strange."

"Strange?" she asked.

"Yes. Like I said, there are so very few of our kind. I'm just surprised that anyone would give up their cygnet. Swans *are* renowned for our pair-bonding, but it's not like we're prudes or anything. If your mother wasn't married or bonded, no one would have shunned her, especially if she were pregnant. At the very least, there are many childless swan couples who would have taken you in."

"R-really?"

"I should hope so." His white brows snapped together. "I'm sorry. Forgive me if I was being too, er, passionate about my defense of our kind. We're very private, which is why we are misunderstood. But I assure you, if you were given up, the circumstances must have been dire."

Hope soared in her chest. All these years ... she was probably right! About her parents having a good reason to give her up. "Dr. Marsh ... I hope you don't think this is too presumptuous of me, but do you think you can ask around ...

maybe your bevy or other bevies if they know about anyone who might have given me up?"

"Of course, Miss Wednesday. I would be happy to ask my bevy mates and reach out to others on your behalf." He patted her arm. "And please, call me Alfie."

"Then you'll have to call me Darcey."

"Darcey, then." He smiled warmly at her. "If you don't mind, Darcey, I think I see an old friend. I'd like to say hello."

"Oh, not at all."

"Cam has my card," he said. "And I have his. May I contact you through him?"

"Of course," she said, nodding excitedly. "Sorry to keep you from your friend."

After they said their goodbyes, she turned to Cam. "Thank you so much. I never dreamed ... I mean, I didn't think I would ever meet another swan much less find the group my parents might have belonged to."

"It was nothing," he said. "Dr. Marsh and I were introduced, and I happened to have mentioned a friend who was a swan. He was quite intrigued because he didn't know of any swan bevies from Las Vegas."

"Still ... it was nice of you to think of me. Thank you."

He shifted uncomfortably. "Would you like to dance?"

"Sure."

She let him lead her to the middle of the dance floor just as the band started a slow tune. Pulling her close, he slipped an arm around her waist, and she reached up to put her hands on his shoulders. As they swayed to the tune, she focused on his handsome face and those unusual eyes behind his glasses, trying to muster up something—anything—other than a friendly warmth.

She sighed internally, and her swan hung its head limply.

Anders's taunting words came back to her. She was tempted

to go home with Cam, if only to prove him wrong, but that wouldn't have been fair to Cam. It felt distasteful to sleep with him, especially knowing what had happened less than an hour ago in the bathroom. She would have to go home alone, and also, tell Cam she couldn't go out with him anymore. Somehow, she knew he wouldn't be too broken up about it.

Damn Anders.

What happened in the bathroom had been a mistake. They'd been caught up in the moment, that was all.

Her swan protested, thwacking its wings at her, but she pushed it deep down inside.

It was the mating bond. Calling to them both. A shudder went through her thinking about Anders's mother. She hadn't been able to control the urge and even left her own son just to be with her mate. It made sense now, how he was.

Oh, Anders. She couldn't find it in herself to hate him. Her heart bled for the little boy who had been abandoned by the first woman he ever loved. She could only hope that one day, he would find peace with himself.

And as for her? Well, there was so much to look forward to now. Maybe she'd find the answers she'd been looking for her entire life. There was still hope for her to be happy, after all.

Chapter 8

Just as she had predicted, Cam wasn't all that upset when she told him after the ball that she didn't have any romantic feelings for him and didn't want to go out with him anymore. Maybe she should have been insulted that he took the news in stride, but honestly, she was more relieved about not having to force an attraction that wasn't there.

He told her, though, he hoped they could remain friends, and she agreed. She liked Cam, despite his cool, aloof nature, and she enjoyed chatting with him. So, it was a surprise to get a call from him just days after the ball. She had just finished ringing up a customer when she saw his name flash on her phone.

"Cam?"

"Hello, Darcey," came his smooth-as-ice voice through the receiver.

Leaning her hip against the counter, she changed the phone to her left hand so she could close up the register. "So ... how's it going? What's up?"

"I'm well," he began. "I wanted to let you know, Dr. Marsh called me."

Her heart leapt in her throat. "What did he say?"

"He wants to meet with you."

"Of course. When? Where? Or should I call him?"

"He said he was free later today, and he was going to have dinner in South Blackstone. He asked if he could meet you for drinks beforehand."

"That would be great. Where?"

"Mickey's Bar and Grill." There was a pause on the other line. "Darcey, I was wondering, if you didn't think it was awkward, perhaps I could come along?"

"You want to come along?"

"Yes. As your friend, of course." There was an emphasis on the word friend. "And, well, I feel responsible."

"Responsible?"

"Yes. I introduced you to Dr. Marsh because I mentioned I knew of another swan shifter, and he was intrigued. But I hadn't met him until that night, and to be honest, I don't really know him. Or what his intentions are."

"He seems like a nice man," she said. "I don't think he has any bad intentions."

"You can't trust what people present to you, Darcey," he said, his tone ominous. "A seemingly benign exterior can be hiding something nefarious."

There was meaning in those words, and curiosity pricked at her. However, they weren't discussing him. "All right."

"Thank you. If anything happened to you, I would never forgive myself."

She blew out a breath. Why did he start saying things like that now? "I'm sure it will be fine. But I know I shouldn't be meeting strangers by myself."

"Perhaps I'm being overly cautious, but as they say, better safe than sorry." He cleared his throat. "I don't have to be there for your conversation, of course. I'm happy to stay back if things get too personal."

"Let's play it by ear, okay?" Looking up at the clock, she made a mental note of how many more hours before she clocked out. "Sarah's closing today, so I'll be done by three, but I have to pick up Adam and bring him home."

"That should work out. I'll tell him we should meet at five thirty?"

"Perfect. Thank you for doing this, Cam."

"Of course, my pleasure, Darcey."

As she put the phone down, she couldn't help but think about Dr. Marsh. He did seem like a sweet, kind man who genuinely wanted to help her. Her swan, too, hadn't picked up anything wrong with him. *Maybe Cam was just being a good friend. A gentleman.*

Which was more than she could say for certain other males.

"Argh!" Placing her elbows on the counter, she rested her chin on her palm. Would there ever be a time when a day, or even a few hours would pass when she didn't think about *him.*

But it really was hard not to think about Anders. Or what had transpired between them. It was like she could still feel his touch. As if his fingers branded her skin permanently. There were moments when she was alone in bed and she grew embarrassingly wet just replaying that night in her head. His naked body, pummeling behind her, into her, while they stared at each other in the mirror. Those golden eyes boring—

"Darcey? Darcey!"

"Huh?" She lifted her head. "Sarah. You're back."

"Yeah," her sister said wryly, lifting her arms to show her the coffees and a brown paper bag in her hands. "Coffee shop was a little busy. Are you all right? You seemed like a million miles away."

"I'm fine." She grabbed one of the coffees and took a sip.

"Just, uh, thinking." She recounted Cam's call to her and told her about the meeting with Marsh.

"Wow." Sarah opened the bag and laid out two pastries. "That's great, Darce. I hope you get some answers."

"Me too." She bit her lip. "You know, whatever happens, you and Adam are still my real family." A few times, Darcey asked if Sarah was ever curious about her biological family. Her sister would just shrug and say that she had tried to locate them, but since she had been abandoned on the side of the road with no clue as to who they were, there was no chance she would ever find them.

Sarah smiled at her warmly and reached out to cover her hand. "Of course, Darcey. I know that. But I know it's not the same, especially because you're a shifter. I'm glad you might get a chance to find out about your biological family."

And she knew Sarah's words were genuine, without a touch of envy or malice. "Thanks, Sarah."

They finished their coffee and pastries quickly, just in time before a couple of customers walked in. Business was brisk today, thankfully, which made the time go by quickly. Soon, she was on her way to pick up Adam. When they got home, she changed into a nicer dress, fancy stiletto boots, and added a scarf to her ensemble.

At five twenty-five she was walking into Mickey's Bar and Grill. Of course, Cam was already by the bar. He waved her over.

"You look lovely, Darcey," he said. "How are you feeling?"

"Good. Nervous," she laughed. "But good."

"Would you like a drink?"

"How about a glass of white wine?" As a shifter, it wouldn't affect her too much, but she liked the taste of wine.

Cam turned to the bartender and ordered her wine. "Thank you letting me be here," he said to her.

"Of course, Cam." Reaching over, she patted his arm. "We're friends, right?"

"Right." A genuine smile lit up his face.

It seemed strange, but Cam was much more relaxed now than he'd ever been on their dates. Initially, she chalked his stiffness to being English, but now she wondered if it was her or maybe the expectations surrounding dating that made him more reserved. Whatever it was, she actually liked this less rigid version of him.

"Darcey, Dr. Spenser."

Turning her head, she saw Alfred Marsh heading their way. "Hello, Alfie," she greeted. "Thanks for contacting Cam and coming to see me."

"Of course." He took off his coat and hung it over his arm. "I'm sorry we have to be brief, but I was hoping you could first tell me more about the circumstances around your adoption before I went and asked around."

"Not a problem." The bartender handed her, her glass of wine, and she took a sip. "I was only a few days old when I was left on the doorstep of the St. Margaret Orphanage in Lund, Nevada. According to the nuns, I was wrapped up in a blanket inside an empty crate of Darcey brand milk." Cam reached over and took her hand into his. Smiling at him gratefully, she continued. "Mother Superior called the police and reported the incident. But they couldn't find any trace of my parents. The orphanage is out in the middle of nowhere, and they didn't have any CCTV cameras on the property. There were no witnesses, and no one in town saw anyone with a baby passing through. When no one came to claim me after a few months, they formally took me in, and I became a ward of the orphanage. Gave me my legal name and got my birth certificate and everything."

"And the nuns didn't know about your shifter nature?"

"No, not until I shifted one day when I was about seven or eight. And to be honest, I didn't even know what I really was until I was eighteen and shifted into my adult form."

Marsh's elegant white eyebrows furrowed together. "Adult form?"

"Yeah. I always thought I'd be a white swan, but it turns out, I'm not. I'm a black swan."

"A black swan." His face fell. "Oh."

"Is there something wrong?"

"Hmm." He scratched at his chin. "I thought you're a mute swan like me. I swore I could tell you were. I hate to tell you this, Darcey, but there are no black swan bevies in North America."

A sinking feeling flooded her stomach. "None? At all?"

He shook his head. "Ever heard the expression *rara avis in terris nigroque simillima cygno*?"

"A rare bird in the lands and very much like a black swan," Cam translated. "From Juvenal. Rome, third—no, second century." His mouth twisted wryly. "Of course, you might also be familiar with the phrase 'husbands without faults, if such black swans there be.'"

"Yes, indeed," Marsh chuckled. "No one thought they existed until Dutch explorers saw them in Western Australia in 1697." His face lit up. "Perhaps that's where you're from. Australia. *Hmm*." He scratched his nose. "I do recall some years ago, our bevy had some guests from there. Perth, if I remember correctly. They were black swans too."

"Do you remember how many years ago?"

His nose twitched. "Not exactly, but it was quite a while ago. Maybe twenty, twenty-five years? I could check with my Alpha to see if he remembers the exact year and their names."

Excitement thrummed in her veins. "If you could, that

would be great. Do you recall if there were any couples with children or anyone pregnant?"

"No, I certainly would remember if they were," he said. "Our visitors were a pair of siblings. The Alpha and his brother."

A dozen scenarios and possibilities whirled in her brain. "Could one of them maybe have mated with someone here in America? Or accidentally gotten a woman pregnant and left to go back?"

"I wouldn't know," Marsh said. "Though those are good theories. I imagine if the Alpha or his brother had gotten a human pregnant and she didn't know what he was or how to contact him, it might have been the reason she gave you up."

A pang of sadness struck her. Maybe her mother was young and struggling and just couldn't afford her. *She loved me,* she convinced herself. *Loved me enough to give me up.*

"Still, those are only theories," Cam reminded them. "Dr. Marsh, you mentioned something about swan pair bonds. What did you mean by that?"

"Oh, yes." Marsh clasped his hands together. "You didn't grow up in a bevy, so you weren't taught this, Darcey."

She cocked her head at him. "Taught what?"

"Swan pair bonds. As you know, swans are known for their fidelity and propensity to mate for life. We spend our lives looking for our mates, and when we do, we bond for life."

"Doesn't that happen for all kinds all shifters?" she asked, thinking of Daniel and Sarah.

"Of course. But you've felt it, haven't you? That keen sense of wanting a mate? That's unique for us swans."

His words struck a chord in her. All this time, she'd wondered why her swan always seemed to be searching for someone to be with.

"For our kind, swan pair bonds are revered above all else,"

Marsh continued. "In fact, only a male who's been fully pair-bonded can rule as Alpha of a bevy. When he dies, then the next strongest mated male becomes Alpha, who may or may not be his offspring."

"Do swans die when their mates pass before them?" Cam asked.

"Ah, I see you've heard the myth about swans dying of heartbreak. While that's been known to happen, many swans can and *do* survive the death of a mate. Our human side, after all, is still in control. Our Alpha, for example, is a widower." He shook his head. "Poor Cassius. He was grief-stricken when Elizabeth died a few years back. She'd been sick for a long time, and we hardly saw her. But he managed to keep it together and still rules our bevy. Oh dear!" Glancing down at his watch, he clucked his tongue. "I'm going to miss my dinner reservation."

"I'm sorry to have kept you," Darcey said.

"No worries, it's only next door." Marsh smiled at her warmly. "It is such a pleasure to meet you, my dear Darcey. A black swan! Imagine. My bevy-mates will be thrilled to hear about you." He took out a card from his pocket and handed it to her. "Drop me a line so I can be in touch."

"Thank you." She took the card from him. "Thank you so much."

"You're very welcome."

As soon as he left, she turned to Cam. "Thanks for coming with me."

"Of course. And you're right, Marsh seems harmless." He shook his head. "I was being paranoid."

"It's fine, Cam," she said. "I'm glad you're here. Um, so I haven't had dinner yet, but do you want to ... get something to eat?"

"That sounds great, Darcey, but I'm afraid I have to run.

There's a species of bat that I've been tracking, and I should go check on the nest I found."

"Oh, no worries then."

"Let me get the check," he said.

"All right, but you'll have to let me pay for my drink since we're friends," she teased.

"Right."

It really was nice that Cam was here, even though her swan didn't like his presence much. It didn't like any male that came near her, and it continued to pine for Anders. *I should have gone home with him,* she thought with regret. At least maybe she could have spent more time with him. Frankly, she was curious if what he said was true. That he could go all night—

What?

Shaking her head mentally, she chided herself. No, she was the New Darcey. *That* was Old Darcey. Or the currently horny Darcey.

"Argh!" Burying her face in her hands, she thought, *God, I'm a mess.*

She wished she had asked Marsh more about swan pair bondings. Were they really stronger than normal shifter matings? Did that mean she could never get rid of this longing for Anders?

"Are you all right?" Cam's voice jolted her out of her thoughts.

"Um, yeah."

"If you don't mind, I need to get going." Cam handed her the black folder from the bartender.

"No prob." She slipped in a couple of bills. "Let's go."

They walked out, and since Cam's black Tesla was right in front of the entrance, he stopped. "Goodnight, Darcey. Drive safe."

"See you." She waved as he got into the driver's side.

Turning on her heel, she walked down half a block to where she parked her car. A stiff autumn breeze blew by, so she tugged her scarf tighter around her.

As she approached her car, a feeling swept over her, and her swan lifted its head. She knew why even before she saw the figure leaning against the hood of her car.

"Hey, Darce," Anders said casually. "You hungry?"

The few days growth of beard on his face only made him more handsome, adding a touch of danger to his aura. Dressed in jeans, a tight white shirt that molded to his broad shoulders and showed off the ink on his arm, he looked more than a snack. He could be her entire meal *and* dessert.

Hungry? That didn't even begin to describe what she was feeling right now.

Chapter 9

Five days, twenty-three hours, twenty-two minutes.

That was the last time Anders saw Darcey, before he walked out of the bathroom where just moments before, he'd been inside her.

He lasted longer than he thought. Staying away from her, not ... being inside her, though that had been embarrassingly quick too. There was no way he could have gone longer, not when it had been years since he'd been with anybody. And Darcey wasn't *just* anybody.

She continued to stare at him like he'd grown a second head. "Darcey?" He waved a hand at her face. "Want to grab a bite to eat?"

Blinking, she shook her head. "Why?"

Now that was a loaded question. "Because it's dinnertime? And I'm starving, and I've had a long day?"

Fucking Damon, sticking him back to day shift *and* trash duty, despite getting all dressed up in that monkey suit and showing up to that stupid ball. Of course, the boss hadn't seen him since he'd made a speedy exit after the encounter in the bathroom, but Anders didn't have the patience to duke it out with the chief. Frankly, his tiger had been moody and unpredictable, and who knows what it would have done.

Sneaking out early today was one of the ways he was getting back at Damon, though he had other motives as well. When he saw Cam walking out of his lab, all dressed up, he just knew he would be going off to see Darcey. Had they already slept together? Or was tonight the night?

It had been eating at him, the thought that she was sleeping with another man. Sure, he all but told her to, but he didn't mean it. He'd been hurt by her refusal to leave with him, and that she wanted to stay at the party—with Cam—after what had just happened.

All his tiger wanted—all *he* wanted—was to have her back in their lair. Safe with them. Away from those people. Specifically, *that woman.* If he ever saw Felicia again, it would be too soon.

"What are you doing here?" Darcey asked, her aquamarine eyes narrowing.

"I was hungry. So, what about it? Dinner?" he asked again. "Unless you and Cam already ate?" He frowned. He saw her arrive in her own car after Cam. Then just now, he left without her. Where was he?

"It's ... it's not like that," she bristled. "He had to leave. But I guess I could eat."

"Hallelujah." Standing up from where he was leaning on her car, he shoved his hands in his jeans. "There's a sushi restaurant not far from here. Is that all right?"

She shrugged. "Lead the way."

He led her a block down toward the restaurant with a sign over the door that said *Shin Nihon* in stylized letters, along with the original *kanji.* Pushing aside the fabric dividers, he let her go inside first.

"*Irasshaimase!*" came the staff's greeting. The cheerful

hostess led them to a booth in the corner, then left them with two menus.

"Have you been here before?" Darcey asked as she perused the menu. "What should I order?"

"Yeah, a couple of times. Food's good, as good as you can get in Colorado, I suppose but not like the real thing."

She raised a brow at him. "You've had *real* Japanese food? Where?"

"In Japan." He opened the menu to the seasonal specials.

"You've traveled to Japan?"

"Just three times. To visit my old sensei in Okinawa."

"Wow."

He peered at her over the folder. "What?"

"I don't even have a passport. And you've been to Japan three times."

"It's no big deal," he said. "Sensei Toyama has a house there, and I stay for two weeks every other summer. Of course, the food here is different from native Okinawan dishes, but then most of the stuff is still excellent."

"Oh, would you mind ordering then?" She put the menu down. "I've had sushi before. And I'm not picky."

"All right, I'll just double my usual." He called the waitress over and rattled off their order. She nodded and then brought them some hot green tea.

She drummed her fingers on the table. "Why did you ask me to dinner?"

He wrapped his fingers around the ceramic cup, feeling the residual heat warm his skin. "This isn't a date."

That might have come out too harsh, but to her credit, she didn't flinch. "I didn't say it was," she shot back.

"We're just eating together," he added.

"Right." She picked off a piece of fluff from her dress. "And you just happened to be waiting by my car tonight?"

"It's a free country, right?"

"Of course."

The waitress thankfully had come back with their starters—boiled edamame, miso soup, and slices of salmon and tuna sashimi. Darcey proceeded to put wasabi in a dish and poured soy sauce into it, then drowned a piece of salmon in the black and green concoction. He couldn't help the sigh that escaped his mouth.

"What now?" she asked in an annoyed tone.

Picking up a piece of sashimi with his chopstick, he popped it into his mouth and ate it in one bite. "All the flavor is in the fish; you don't need soy sauce or wasabi. But if you do"—he took the tiniest smudge of wasabi and placed it on one end of a slice, then picked it up and lightly dipped the edge in the soy sauce —"this is how you do it."

"All right, sensei." She rolled her eyes and then repeated what he did.

As she popped the fish into her mouth and chewed thoughtfully, he couldn't help but stare at her plump lips, remember how they felt and tasted. How her body fit so perfectly against his and her soft skin—

"Oh." She swallowed. "That is good."

Pushing those earlier thoughts aside, he smirked at her. "See? You gotta trust me on this."

"All right." She put her hands up. "Show me your ways, master."

As dinner proceeded, Anders found himself having a good time. He liked seeing her smile, loved hearing her talk. She told him about growing up with the nuns and Sarah and Adam, while she also asked him about the community center.

"So, you've been going there forever?" she asked as they ate their dessert of mochi and green tea ice cream.

"Since I was ... oh, about nine years old," he said. "Mary was one of my neighbors, and so after school, I'd ride over with her. I wanted to take up basketball, but their slots were filled while there were only a few kids signing up for karate. I felt like a nerd dressing up in that uniform, but hey, turns out kicking boards and smashing concrete blocks were a lot of fun." Not to mention, it helped him get out his aggression, among other things. If it wasn't for the community center and Toyama, well ... he might have taken that hostility out on someone else. "By the way, I thought Adam was going to start volunteering?"

"Yeah, he's definitely going to, but he's still getting settled in school."

"How's that going?"

"I think he's actually fitting in well. No more bullies, from what I can tell. And except for having to wake up early, he doesn't dread going into school every day."

"Lucas Lennox is a great high school," he said. "Oh, there's gonna be a few bad apples, but for the most part, everyone's cool. He's just got to be able to hold his own. I meant what I said, by the way, about him taking karate. I can look into how to modify the *katas* for him or ask my sensei for help."

Her hand stopped halfway as she was about to put a spoonful of ice cream in her mouth. "Really? You would do that for him?" Her pretty aquamarine eyes widened.

"Why not? He's a good kid, despite that smart mouth." He could see a little bit of himself in Adam. That aggression, yes, but also grit and determination.

"I'll ask him when he wants to start coming in." She put her spoon down and stared down at her lap.

An awkward silence stretched between them. *God, why was this so hard?* Being around her was both difficult and easy. Easy because it felt so right. Difficult because there was so much he wanted to say and do but couldn't.

"I'm sorry," he blurted out.

Her head whipped up. "Sorry? For what?"

"If I make things difficult. You don't have to avoid me at the center if you and Adam want to volunteer. God knows they could use all the help they can get. I'm sure we can find a way so it won't be awkward."

"Oh." She sounded almost disappointed. "Thanks."

He signaled for the waitress and handed her a couple of bills. "*Arigatō gozaimashita.*" She nodded and smiled, then walked away. "We should go. I'll walk you to your car."

"Wait, did you just pay? How much—"

Not bothering to wait for her, he slid out of the booth and out of the door. Darcey followed behind him, her stiletto boots clicking on the pavement. He slowed down, allowing her to catch up beside him, and they walked silently toward her car.

"Thanks for dinner," she said as she reached into her purse for her keys. "You really should have let me pay my share."

"Yeah, whatever." He shoved his hands into his pockets.

Taking her keys out, she unlocked her door and opened it. However, instead of going inside, she turned back to him. "And I'm sorry too."

"For what?"

"For not coming home with you that night." Desire glittered in her eyes, making his stomach clench. But before he could say anything, she slipped inside.

Shock coursed through his system. He couldn't think or speak or move. He just stood there, watching her car drive farther and farther away, the rear lights turning to pinpoints before finally disappearing.

His pulse pounded madly. That smoldering flame he saw in her eyes startled him, but he didn't doubt that he'd seen it. His tiger roared, spurring him on to *go after her*!

Sprinting to his car, he quickly got in and started the engine. His body was on autopilot as he drove down the road. He caught up with her just as she was taking a left onto the main road out of South Blackstone.

Not wanting to scare her, he stayed behind a good distance. *This was crazy,* he kept telling himself. Yet, he kept chasing after her, a sense of urgency propelling him forward. His tiger relished the hunt and egged him on.

Finally, they were on a suburban street. It was quiet and dark, save for the streetlamps and the lights from the houses. Darcey pulled up to a sprawling, two-story house, parking her car behind the red van he'd seen her drive at the center. His heart threatened to leap out of his chest when she got out of the car and headed inside.

He circled around and parked a few houses down. As he cut the engine, he stared at the house. Waiting. Watching. But for what, he didn't know. *I should go.* But he made no motion to start the truck. When the lights in the house turned off, he got out.

Quietly, steadily, he crept around the back. The fence wasn't so high, so he easily scaled it and landed on his feet gracefully. Cutting across the backyard and rounding the swimming pool, he approached the house. The walls of the entire ground floor consisted of glass doors.

A movement caught his eye and he went still. In the corner room, he saw a figure drawing the curtains. The light from the room was enough for him to see a shadow. A feminine shadow. Then the room went dark.

Now or never.

Darting across the grass, he made a beeline for the room. He reached for the handle to test that it was locked. Unfortunately, he didn't anticipate it being unlocked, and the glass door slid aside with a loud thud.

Shit!

He stepped inside and scrambled to reach the door handle,

pushing the curtains aside so he could grab it and put it back in place. Slowly, he turned around, ready to confront an outraged Darcey—or possibly a rampaging grizzly bear who heard him break into its den.

However, he was not prepared for the sight that greeted him as his eyes adjusted to the darkness. "Darcey?"

There she was, lying across the bed, waves of white-blonde hair like a halo around her, wearing only a black lace bustier, panties, garters, and stockings. A smile spread across her lips, her aquamarine eyes twinkling knowingly.

She knew I was coming for her. "Minx," he muttered under his breath.

She sat up, patting the mattress invitingly. "Are you just going to stand there?"

He didn't need to be told twice.

As he stalked to the bed, he shucked his shirt off, followed by his boots, socks, and jeans. He crawled on the mattress toward her, and she met him halfway, her arms opening to embrace him.

"Darcey." A sizzle of electricity went up his spine the moment their bodies touched. He leaned down to kiss her, but she stopped him with a finger to his lips.

"We have to be quiet," she said in a low voice. "Adam's in the room at the end, and Sarah and Daniel are above us."

The corner of his lips tugged up and he kissed her finger. "This is a shifter household, beautiful. If my guess is correct, each room has been thoroughly soundproofed."

Her delicate brows knitted together. "How do you know?"

"Because the lights are off all over the house, and I can't hear a damned thing. Have you heard a single peep with your enhanced hearing the entire time you've been here? Do you think Daniel and Sarah have been up there just sleeping every night?"

"Oh. Right." Her arms snaked around his neck. "Carry on, then."

He leaned forward and captured her sweet mouth, her distinct taste and smell flooding his senses, and he licked and sucked at her lips. He made a motion to push her down on the mattress, but to his surprise, she managed to leverage her weight, and he found himself on his back as she straddled him. When he tried to sit up, her hands stopped him.

"Nuh-uh," she tsked and shook a finger at him. "Stay. Down."

Motherloving Christ.

Her hips rocked against his growing erection as she leaned down, her hair falling over her shoulders to tickle his skin. She pressed a feather-light kiss on his mouth, then on his sternum. Soft, delicate hands caressed his shoulders, her eyes glowing appreciatively. Obviously, she liked what she saw. Leaning lower, she trailed her mouth over his chest and down to his abs. When her hands reached for his boxers and pulled them down to his thighs, he gritted his teeth.

She let out a gasp as his erection sprang free, but reached for him with eager hands. Her palm encircled him firmly, her fingers exploring the length of him.

"Oh. God." He threw his head back as she began to stroke him. The pressure of her hand was just right, the speed and rhythm steady. He felt her move again, and when something warm and wet enveloped him, he let out a loud groan and grabbed a fistful of sheets.

God, she looked amazing. Her hair spilling over his thighs. Eyes closed. Pink, lush lips wrapped around his cock. As if he wasn't already overstimulated, she opened her eyes and looked straight at him, pure lust in her gaze.

Fuck. He didn't want to watch her for fear of blowing his load right there, but he couldn't turn away either. Each stroke and lick and suck brought him closer to the edge. And all he could do was watch.

"Darcey!" He thrust his fingers into her hair, guiding her. Slowing her down, just enough to stop him from going over, but still sending zings of pleasure up and down his spine. Unable to take it, he pulled her away, then flipped their positions.

She let out a squeaky chuckle as he covered her body with his. "Naughty little bird," he growled against her mouth. "I'm going to punish you."

"Are you going to spank me?"

He wasn't thinking of that, though it did sound like a good idea. Later, he told himself. For now, he needed her. To be inside her again. He pushed his boxers all the way off and tossed them aside.

Reaching for the front of her bustier, he pulled it down to reveal her perfect, bountiful breasts. He reached for her lace panties, but there was no way to take them off without removing the garter and stockings. *Damn, and I wanted another souvenir.* So, he ripped the lace to shreds.

"Hey!" she protested. "I liked those."

"I'll get you more," he said, positioning himself between her spread thighs. "As many as you want. I'll buy out your whole damned store."

"I—oh!" Her lips parted as he nudged against her. He teased her clit with the head of his cock until she was moaning and gasping. Replacing his tip with his finger, he circled her nub as he slowly inched inside her.

"Oh. God. Yes," she said in a breathy tone.

He filled her up, seating himself fully inside her. Hauling one of her knees up, he pushed further, making her cry out as he thrust in deep.

Closing his eyes, he moved slow. The last time had been frantic, full of excitement, but too quick. He wanted to feel her, languish in the feeling of being inside her, so he took long, leisurely strokes.

She groaned, her hips lifting up to meet his, urging him to move faster. *Not yet.* He gritted his teeth, wanting this feeling to last longer.

He picked up the pace, leaning down so he could kiss her mouth, her neck, everywhere. Her legs wrapped around him as her hands roamed, touching his face, his shoulders, trailing down his back. He buried his face in her neck, inhaling her scent deep, like a drug he couldn't get enough of.

"Yes, yes," she moaned against his ear as he ground into her deeper.

Their moans, sighs, and groans filled the room, the sounds of their lips and skin slapping together like an erotic symphony. He held her tighter against him and pummeled into her. Kissing and licking every bit of skin he could reach as her body shuddered with pleasure. But he wasn't satisfied with just one orgasm. No, he continued, reaching down between them to pluck at her clit, while continuing to fuck into her.

"Yes, that's it, beautiful," he urged between thrusts, pushing her higher and higher until he felt her squeeze him tight. He gave her half a second to recover before he rocked into her again.

He stared down, deep into her aquamarine eyes, and she looked back, eyes glittering with lust as her body clenched around him.

Her orgasm set off his own, her sweet pussy milking his aching cock. He let out a long grunt as he thrust deep, feeling his balls drain dry as he came, filling her up. His vision turned white briefly, and spine-tingling pleasure coursed through his body before he collapsed on top of her.

"Oh. Jesus. Beautiful." Air finally decided to enter his lungs, and he took a deep breath. "God." It took another few seconds for him to recover enough to slip out of her and roll over to his back.

Looking over at her, he saw Darcey, too, was breathing deeply, her eyes closed. Her full breasts heaved, and her skin glowed as a sheen of sweat covered her gorgeous, naked body. He could look at her all day, with or without lingerie on. Reaching out, he curled an arm around her and pressed her to his side.

She didn't protest, and instead, cuddled closer. He stared up at the ceiling, and as the post-orgasmic bliss ebbed away, questions began to seep into his mind. His chest tightened, so he pushed those thoughts away. "I should go," he blurted out.

Yawning, she covered her mouth with her hand. "You should."

What? "I just don't ... I never stay the night." Technically true.

"I didn't mistake you for the type." Stretching her arms over her head, she rolled over to the other side and pulled a pillow to her. "Don't forget to close the door on your way out."

Sliding off the bed, he grabbed his jeans, hopped into them, and gathered the rest of his clothes. Glancing back at her, he waited for a heartbeat, but she didn't stir. From her even breathing, he could tell she had fallen asleep. He reached for the door handle and headed out into the cool, dark night.

A pit formed in his stomach, and his tiger growled with indignation. He told himself this was what he needed to do and grabbed his tiger by the scruff and told it to shut the hell up.

He couldn't get attached to her or get too close. The urge to claim her was there, lurking in the depths of his mind, now, ready to pounce.

But he would never give in, not to his animal urges. He would never bond with anyone.

This was what he wanted, right?

Chapter 10

Darcey opened her eyes the moment she heard the door close.

This was what she wanted, right?

With a deep sigh, she slipped under the covers, hugging her pillow closer. The cool fabric was nothing like Anders's hot, hard body, which only moments ago had been on top of her giving such mindless pleasure that she had to bite her lip from crying out words that she might regret later.

Her swan trilled sadly at the loss of his presence.

"Nuh-uh." She shook a finger at her swan. This was the New Darcey, right? Had she forgotten her goal of becoming strong and independent, of not needing any man to boost her self-worth or bend over backwards to please them? She got what she wanted from Anders, and now ... now ...

Well, now, she didn't know what to do. Actually, she'd never gotten to this part of any relationship. Usually by this time, she'd be the one coaxing him to stay. Then as her usual cycle progressed, she'd follow up with a week of non-stop texts and calls until she got the "let's just be friends" or "I'm not ready for a relationship" chat. Or worse, got ghosted. But, no, she wasn't going to do that anymore.

Somehow, she thought that being on the other side would be better.

Punching her pillow, she turned to the other side and closed her eyes. *New Darcey*, she reminded herself. Newer and better Darcey.

When she opened her eyes, it was already light out. As she got out of bed, a feeling crept over her. A sense of emptiness, which only pervaded as she showered and readied herself for the day. When she picked up one of her stockings from between the sheets, the co-mingled scents of Anders, her, and sex drifted into her nose, and another pang hit her. Ignoring it, she tossed her stockings into her laundry basket and left the room.

It was Saturday, meaning she didn't have to drop off Adam to school, so she went about her day, taking a long, leisurely brunch at Rosie's. She was closing today, so she would be heading into work later. She and Sarah had found a good working rhythm where one of them opened and the other closed. It left them both leisure time during the day which was important now as days off were impossible with the business still being new. Hopefully in a couple of weeks they could afford to hire someone part time and they could each have a day off, and eventually, Sarah could go on a long-delayed honeymoon with Daniel.

After she finished paying for food, she popped into the back to say hi to Temperance and Gabriel, then headed for the exit.

"Excuse me!" She exclaimed as she bumped into someone who was coming into the cafe. A pair of hands grabbed her arms to steady her. "Sorry."

"No worries, young lady."

She peered up at the source of the voice. It was an older man, probably in his sixties, with light blue eyes that pierced into her. "I wasn't, uh, looking at where I was going." A strange shiver ran down her spine.

The blue-eyed man was tall and slim, wearing an impeccable pin stripe suit, his white hair slicked back against his skull. His unnerving gaze never left hers. "Neither was I."

"Uh, all right then." She shrugged out of his grasp. "Excuse me." As she left the cafe, that shiver lingered on. That other man had been a shifter, for sure, but living in Blackstone meant she was surrounded by them. It didn't faze her anymore when she met them, and she no longer spent her time trying to figure out what they were.

Putting it out of her mind, she drove to Silk, Lace, and Whispers stopping by the cafe to grab Sarah a mid-morning coffee. The boutique was busy, for which Darcey was glad as she barely had time to think. Even more customers came in when Sarah took off to pick up Adam, which meant by the time she was closing up at six-thirty, her feet were sore, and she was mentally exhausted.

"Whew!" she exclaimed loudly as she turned the Open sign to Closed. Still, each week continued to be their best one yet in terms of sales. SLW was a hit among the women—and men—of Blackstone.

She finished some work in the office, closed up the boutique, then locked up and headed to her parked car. With the weather turning fully into fall, it was already dark even though it wasn't very late. As she entered the parking lot, a strange sensation swept over her, and her swan lifted its neck and flapped its wings.

Danger, it almost seemed to say.

Something large whipped by next to her, but it went so fast that she didn't see what it was. As her heart pounded a mad rhythm in her chest, she ran toward her car. *Keep it together, keep it together*, she repeated to herself. But her hands were shaking so hard, she dropped her purse when she tried to grab her keys. Before she could bend down to pick it up, a pair of hands grabbed her upper arms from behind.

"Let go of me!" she shrieked as she attempted to shrug off her attacker. "I said—"

"Shh ... Darcey, it's me."

She froze, recognizing the voice, and the fear she felt earlier melted away.

"Hey ..." Anders cooed, turning her around to face him. Golden honey eyes peered down at her, full of concern. "What's wrong—*oomph!*"

She launched herself into his embrace, unable to help herself. His scent, his warm body, and his presence calmed her and her swan down. Strong arms came around her and soothed her back as she pressed her cheek on his chest.

"Darcey ... beautiful ... it's all right."

Now that she was calmer, embarrassment replaced the adrenaline and fear. "I ... I'm sorry." She pulled away from him. "I'm being silly. I—"

"No, you weren't." He gripped her arms again. "What's wrong? Did something scare you?"

She forced a laugh. "No. I mean, it was probably the wind. It just felt like someone ran right by me. Um, did you see anything?"

He shook his head. "No, I was inside." He pointed his chin at his pickup truck which was parked next to her car. "Was someone following you? Watching you?"

"I didn't see anyone." She wrinkled her nose. "What are you doing here?"

"I ... uh ..." He scratched at his head.

Her traitorous little heart beat madly—this time, at the thought that he was here for *her*. "Can we go somewhere, please?"

"Sure. Where?"

"Anywhere but here." There was still a chill in the air, and a feeling swept over her, telling her that things weren't quite right.

"All right." Placing an arm around her, he led her to his truck, opening the door to let her in.

As she settled in, she placed her forehead against the cool window. Anders got into the driver's seat, and soon, they were off.

She wasn't sure how long they had been driving or where they were going, but eventually he stopped and pulled up to a cabin-style, double-wide trailer. "Where are we?"

"My place," he said, turning off the engine. "C'mon, I'll make you a drink, and you can just sit until you feel better."

Slipping out of the truck, she followed him up toward the front door. There were no other houses around, and they seemed to be in the woods somewhere. "Where are we?" she asked.

"Blackstone Mountains," he answered. "On the east side, near the bottom. A large patch of land is reserved for housing for rangers who want to be near work. Anyone who's got at least five years can apply, and they make it easy for you to own your own place." He opened the door and let her go in. "Make yourself comfortable," he said before heading toward the kitchen island.

It was hard not to stare and soak in the interior of his trailer, because this wasn't the type of place she'd imagined him to be living in. It was spacious and modern, but very minimally decorated. Aside from the armchair, couch, and coffee table, the only decoration in the room was a paper divider in the corner and a shelf with a few knickknacks. The first thing that caught her eye as she walked closer was the single photo on the shelf. It was of Anders and an older Japanese man with white hair and weathered skin, dressed in Hawaiian shirts, standing in clear blue water to their ankles, and two large rocks behind them.

"That's in Okinawa. *Kouri* island."

Anders sudden appearance beside her made her start, and she stepped away from the shelf like a kid being caught doing something naughty. "I'm sorry, I didn't—"

"No, it's fine." A fond smile spread across his face. "Sensei Toyama brought me there the first time I visited. Those are called the heart rocks."

"Heart rocks?" she echoed.

"Yeah, they're shaped like hearts, see?"

Squinting at the photo, she could make out the shape. "Oh. Right."

"Tea?" He handed her one of the two cups he held in his hands.

"Thanks."

He walked over to the couch, and she followed, sitting on the other end from him. Lifting the cup to her lips, she took a sip. The tea tasted similar to what they had at the Japanese restaurant last night, but had a nuttier flavor. "Thank you for the tea."

"You're welcome." His expression turned serious. "Now, what scared you?"

"I'm not ... it's silly." She shrugged. "Probably the wind."

"You didn't see anything? No one's been around you, following you? Or have any more of your admirers popped up?" His knuckles grew white as they tightened around his cup.

"Uh, no." That damned billboard. "By the way, I told Sarah I wanted it to come down as soon as our rental on it expires. Or at least replace the photo with a professional model."

"Look." He place his cup on the coffee table. "I didn't mean to make it sound like you were asking for it. You should be free to do what you want with your body without worrying about having creeps coming after you."

She set her cup down next to his. "Then why were you so angry that time? Was it so awful?"

"No, *you* were absolutely stunning. But I didn't want anyone else to see you like that. Not ... not when *I* hadn't seen you like that."

A breath caught in her throat as he stared at her with those golden eyes. "Anders, I—"

He made the first move this time, pouncing on her as his arms came around her. Desire flared in her as their lips touched, his kisses becoming hungrier each second.

She found herself being lifted up and carried into the bedroom at the end. Clothes were shed urgently, more kisses were exchanged, and she forgot about her troubles as they were replaced with the desperate need to be close to him. To have him inside her.

The sex was slow and unhurried, yet still laced with a hunger that couldn't be sated. He took his time exploring her body, and she did too. When they finally reached that last crescendo, they held each other tight, mouths melded together, as if afraid to let go.

How long they stayed fused, she didn't know. Her eyes closed, and she drifted for a bit, waking only when he rolled off her.

Her mind was only beginning to process what had happened when she heard a familiar ring tone. Jolting up, she scrambled off the bed and out to the living room, making a grab for her phone. "Yes?"

"Darce?" came Adam's voice. "Where are you?"

She glanced at the clock. It was past eight. "Still here. I'm, uh, having car trouble."

"Why didn't you call? I thought we were doing pizza and a movie while Sarah and Daniel went out on a date night."

Crap! "My phone ran out of juice, and I'm just charging it now." She sprinted back to the bedroom to grab her clothes from the floor, unable to look at Anders. "I'm on my way. Why don't you go ahead and order the pizza, then it'll be there by the time I get back?"

"Yeah, sure. Did you want to watch an action flick or a comedy."

Holding the phone to her ear with her shoulder, she hopped into her panties. "Either's fine."

"'Kay. See you in a bit, Darce."

"See you."

"Who was that?" Anders stood up, frowning as she bent down to pick up her bra.

"Adam." She slipped her arms into the straps and clipped it on in the back. "He's home alone, and I forgot I was supposed to hang out with him while Sarah and Daniel went out."

His expression relaxed. "Oh. Uh—"

"Do you think I can call a cab from here?" She put on the rest of her clothes and ran her fingers through her hair.

"I'll take you back to your car."

"No time." She rushed back out to the living room to grab her purse.

"I'll take you home then."

Her brain told her to say no, but she couldn't waste any more time, not when she'd left Adam waiting. "I—Fine." She could get a ride back to the boutique tomorrow.

He got dressed quickly and led her out to his truck. Anxiety filled her at the thought of Adam by himself, which was good, because that meant she didn't have to think about what just happened.

Soon, they were pulling up to the front of the house. Thank

goodness Sarah and Daniel were out and Adam was probably already settled in the living room. "Um, thanks for the ride."

Before she could open the door, a hand settled on her shoulder. "Darcey, we should—"

"Come by tomorrow night," she said quickly, unable to stop the words from leaving her mouth. "I'll leave the door unlocked again."

Without a backward glance, she sprinted toward the front door, her heart still pounding as she entered the house. Had she really said those words? Would he even show up tomorrow?

———

He showed up that following night. And the one after that. Two weeks passed, and they had spent nearly every night in each other's arms. However, as if by silent agreement, neither of them stayed afterwards. She told herself it was better this way as she didn't want Sarah, Daniel, or God forbid, Adam finding out. But part of her didn't want to admit that she'd been starting to feel things she didn't want to feel.

Each time she told herself it would be the last. Her swan protested, wanting to be near him all the time, and she found herself succumbing to temptation. He was too irresistible, and not like the men in her past. While she had pined for them, she actually craved Anders.

Maybe tonight will be the last night, she thought as she worked on the window display in the shop. But then again, that's what she kept saying every night, but somehow, she still ended up sleeping with him.

Today was a slow Wednesday afternoon, plus it was dark and drizzling outside, so there was hardly any traffic. Normally she was thankful for the downtime, but it was hard to keep busy when no one came in. And when she let her mind wander, it only went to one thing. Or one person.

As if on cue, her phone chirped with a text.

Hey, beautiful.

Her heart skipped a beat. *Hey, yourself,* she typed back.

See you tonight.

She bit her lip, staring at the message. As she began to type out a reply, something caught her eye outside the shop—a familiar, white-haired man walking by. *Alfred Marsh.* She'd been so distracted these last two weeks, she hadn't even thought of him or called him back. Slipping her phone into her pocket, she dashed out the door.

"Alfie!" she called out. "Dr. Marsh!"

The man turned around, brows knitted together, but when they locked eyes, he went pale and turned on his heel, picking up his pace as he continued to walk away.

"Wait!" She was about to chase after him, but two women walked into the shop. *Crap!* With a last glance at Marsh's retreating back, she went inside. *How weird.* But there was no time to unpack what just happened.

"Hi," she said to the women. "Can I help you, ladies?"

The rest of the afternoon went slowly, as the rain continued to fall and it grew gloomier outside. Anticipation thrummed in her veins as six thirty came closer and closer. She finished some work in the office and then practically flew out the door to rush home.

Even as she ate dinner with Adam and Sarah, her mind kept drifting to Anders. She volunteered to do the dishes as she needed the distraction.

Finally, as she lay in bed wearing a sexy new negligee, the sound of the back door sliding open made her jump off the bed.

"Hi," she said as she rushed up to meet him. Heat coiled in her stomach as she soaked up the sight of his damp, tousled hair and the tight T-shirt stretched over his tanned, muscled skin as he entered the room.

"Hi, yourself," he greeted back, his gaze already greedily soaking up her body.

"Um, did you eat yet?"

Golden honey eyes burned with desire. "I'm hungry, but not for food."

Oh, mercy me.

Chapter 11

Anders swore Damon must still be pissed at him, because he seemed to be getting the short end of the stick at work lately. Some punk kids thought it would be funny to set fire to bags of poop in the middle of the woods. But they didn't use dog poop like normal people. No, they had to use large bags of buffalo poop, each the size of a garbage can. Unfortunately, the wind must have changed direction, and the flames jumped into a pile of dead leaves, making the fire spread. Thankfully they had contained the fire just in time, but it had been a close call.

Talk about a shit job. That damned smoke was so foul, he'd basically have to toss out his uniform. Everyone gave him a wide berth as he entered HQ and headed to the lockers.

He was dirty and exhausted, and as he stood under the hot spray of the water in the shower room, his mind drifted to Darcey. Every minute he wasn't with her, she was on his mind. She and her sweet, curvy body, lush lips, and smooth skin. *Shit.* If he wasn't careful, he'd have a full-blown erection in front of the other guys.

Who could blame him? The sex with Darcey was phenomenal, and he craved for her every moment of the day.

Sneaking around and leaving right after, though, that didn't settle well with him. But they had an unspoken understanding, and neither brought up the subject of what they were doing and where this was going. He attempted to stay away from her, but who the hell was he kidding? With a girl like Darcey, one or two or three times would never be enough. The thought of not being able to hold her and kiss her made his chest tighten.

Shutting off the water, he toweled off and got dressed. Those two clowns—Gilmore and Davis—were in the locker area and gave him wary glances before they headed out. *Good.* Word must have gotten around about the postcard incident, and he hadn't seen anyone else put Darcey's picture in their lockers.

Only a couple more hours before he could see her. He'd been careful whenever he snuck into Daniel's house. It was tough, because they both worked the same shifts now, so he drove slower, and made sure the bear shifter got home first before parking his car a few houses away and sneaking into the backyard. Thankfully, Daniel was distracted enough with his own mate that he hadn't caught Anders these last two weeks.

"Anders."

He froze. Damon. "What can I do for you, Chief?"

Damon cleared his throat. "Good work out there. On the fires."

Wow, was Damon actually complementing him today? "All part of the job. Didja need me for anything else? I have to get back to work."

"F.D.'s still clearing up that sector so they're not letting anyone in. Look, you've had a hard morning. Why don't you take the rest of the day off?"

His jaw practically unhinged itself. "You're shitting me?"

Damon chuckled. "I think you've already been shit on enough today. Go on, before I change my mind."

He wasn't one to look this gift horse in the mouth. "Thanks,

Chief," he said with a two-fingered salute before he pivoted toward the exit. He fished his truck keys out of his pocket, making a beeline for his parking spot. As he grabbed the handle to the driver's door, a voice from behind made him freeze.

"Anders? Anders Stevens?"

Dropping his hand to his side, he turned around. His heart slammed into his rib cage as he stared back at familiar golden-brown eyes. Eyes that belonged to *him*. Felicia's son. "Yeah, kid?"

Today he was dressed more casually in a dark sweater, checkered shirt, khakis, and a suede jacket. He still reeked of *eau de la rich preppy kid.*

"I'm Christopher," he said. "We met at Blackstone Castle a couple of weeks ago."

"Yeah? And so?"

His lips pursed together. "How do you know my mother?"

"I don't."

"I don't believe that," he shot back.

"You heard what she said," Anders snorted. "I'm *nobody.*"

But Christopher pressed on. "You're a tiger, right? So am I, but my dad's a lynx shifter. Clive Kerr."

Just the sound of the name made his blood boil and sent his tiger pacing. "Good for you." He turned to get into his car, but a hand on his shoulder stopped him. He whipped around, shrugging off the touch. "What do you want from me, kid?"

Christopher swallowed hard. "The truth. About who you are."

He shut his eyes tight and turned back to his truck. "Go ask your mother." Without another word, he hopped into his pickup and shut the door. He could still feel Christopher's eyes on him, but he ignored it and instead, started the engine and pulled out of his spot.

Fuck Christopher. Fuck Felicia. And fuck my Goddamn life.

He let out a growl as he sped down the mountain road, his rage barely contained. That kid ... what was he thinking, confronting him like that? Did he really want to open this can of worms? Anders didn't need this shit right now.

His body was still vibrating with emotions by the time he reached home. "Goddammit!" He slammed his palms on the wheel. His tiger was on edge, too, prowling back and forth, body tensed like a tightly-wound spring.

Jesus. There was no doubt in his mind that Felicia would have children with her mate, but that had always been an abstract idea to him. To be confronted with the fact was a completely different matter. How old was Christopher? Did he have siblings? How many, and what were they?

"Fuck." He couldn't think of that, or it would slowly drive him insane. It was hard to breathe, as his chest was collapsing in on itself. He needed something to distract him. To anchor him.

Darcey.

She was the first thing that popped into his head. He needed to see Darcey and her sweet smile and beautiful face. He didn't care if he had to show up at the boutique or if Sarah was there. He needed to touch her, smell her, embrace her. It would be the only balm that could soothe this ache growing inside him.

Chapter 12

Darcey wouldn't have thought anything about Marsh's strange behavior except that her instinct kept telling her something was not right. She remembered he gave her his card, so she called him several times, but his number was unreachable. She tried texting, too, but there was no answer. It had been a week since that incident, and she still couldn't figure it out. A pit in her stomach began to form. From her unfortunate previous experiences with men, she knew when her number was being blocked.

"You okay, Darce?"

Daniel's voice jolted her out of her thoughts. They were all sitting at the breakfast table, finishing up their breakfast. "Yeah? I mean, yes."

"Not hungry?" Sarah nodded at the plate in front of her, where she had taken two bites out of her pancakes.

"Just a little queasy today," she said.

"You do look a little green around the gills," Sarah remarked. "Are you sick?"

"Uh, yeah. My stomach hasn't been well lately." Not since that day Marsh ran away from her. He had clearly seen her, but something had scared him. She woke up in the mornings, feeling nauseated. *What could have happened?*

Daniel looked at her strangely. "You're sick?"

"Can I have your pancakes?" Adam asked before her brother-in-law could say anything more.

"Sure." She pushed her plate at him. "I'm not really hungry. Excuse me." She got up from the table and headed into her room to finish getting ready.

She wished she could talk to Anders about it, but they hardly spoke when they were together those brief hours of the night. Truth be told, she didn't want any conversation during that time anyway lest she accidentally blurt out things she would regret later. Somehow, she could tell he felt the same, like they had some kind of silent agreement to keep things physical. She would not break that, no matter how much her swan protested.

If only there was someone she could talk to about the whole Marsh and the Australian bevy situation. She didn't want to bother Sarah and Daniel over it, but no one knew the situation like her and—

Cam.

She'd nearly forgotten about him. *Maybe he knew what was up with Marsh.* Dialing his number, she sat on the bed, waiting for him to pick up. There was no answer, so she waited and tried again. Two more unanswered calls, and she finally left a voice message. "Hey, Cam, it's me. Darcey. I, uh, wanted to talk to you about something. I just don't know how to ask you. Anyway, give me a call back when you can. No rush."

With a deep sigh, she put the phone down and went to the bathroom. After washing her face and changing her top, she left the house, then drove to the boutique to open it up for the day. Sarah came in before noon, but she wasn't alone. Following behind her was Cam.

"Oh, hey, Cam," she greeted.

"Good morning, Darcey." He looked perfectly handsome as usual with his gold-rimmed glasses and crisp white shirt rolled up to his elbows. However, her stomach didn't do that flippy-thing like it did when she saw Anders. *Oh God.* Last night when he did that thing with his finger—

"Hello? Earth to Darcey?" Sarah waved a hand at her face. "Are you sure you're not sick? You can go home if you want."

"What? No, no, I'm fine." She turned to Cam. "What are you doing here?"

"I saw your missed calls and listened to your message," he said. "Terribly sorry. I had to turn off my phone. I was observing a nest of blue jays, so I didn't want to be disturbed."

"You could have called me back," she said with a chuckle.

"It sounded urgent, so I thought I'd pop by." He actually looked concerned. "You said you wanted to ask me something?"

"Uh ..." She bit her lip.

Sarah cleared her throat. "Darce, why don't you take an early lunch break?"

"But—"

"It's fine, I can manage for a while," her sister urged.

"All right, thanks, Sarah. Cam?"

"Let's go to the Japanese restaurant around the corner," he suggested as they left the boutique. "I heard the food was good."

"Er, how about something else?" Going to that place with anyone else but Anders seemed like a betrayal. Besides, the thought of raw fish right now made her want to barf again. "I don't want to take a lot of your time, so why don't we grab a sandwich at the cafe?"

"As you like."

The cafe was packed as it was lunchtime, so Cam suggested she save them a seat outside while he got them their food. When he came back, he handed her a sandwich and iced tea. "Thanks."

"So," he began as he took a sip of his tea. "What did you need to ask me?"

"It's about Alfie. Dr. Marsh." She relayed to him what happened outside SLW last week and about him blocking her number. "Have you heard from him? Did he say anything about me or the black swan bevy?"

"Hmmm." He rubbed his chin with his thumb and forefinger. "I'm sorry, Darcey, I haven't heard from him. A mutual acquaintance introduced us at the ball because Marsh is an entomologist, then when he told me about being a swan, I mentioned you. Other than that time and Mickey's, I haven't been in contact with him."

"Oh." Her shoulders sank.

"I don't know why he would block you or even run away, if you are certain that was him you saw." He reached over to cover her hand with his. "But I can find out."

"Really? That's nice of you, Cam."

"Of course. We're friends, after all."

She smiled at him. "Right. And, uh, I'm sorry I haven't called or anything. Except for asking a favor."

"It's all right, I've been busy too," he said. "Well, we're here now, so we can make up for lost time."

They spent the rest of the hour talking, mostly about work. There was still that niggling feeling in the back of her brain that bothered her, but at least for now, she was distracted. When they were done, they got up and headed to the boutique, Cam's hand on the small of her back as they chatted.

"... of course, the moment I got up close enough to that nest, the branch began to break and—" Cam stopped suddenly. "Oh, hello. Fancy running into you here, Stevens."

Darcey froze, then slowly turned her head toward the

direction Cam nodded. Sure enough, Anders stood in their path.

"Dr. Spenser," he greeted coolly before his gaze flickered at her. "Darcey."

"What are you doing here?" she blurted out. "I mean ... uh ..."

"Heading out to eat." His jaw clenched.

"That's nice." She hoped her tone sounded as casual as she thought it did.

"Looks like you guys had a nice lunch," he bit out. "Come here often, Doc?"

Cam bristled. "I should get back to work."

"You should," Anders said, nostrils flaring.

"Me too." She swallowed hard, feeling her stomach roil again.

"See you around, Stevens."

She forced herself to keep looking forward as Cam led her back to the boutique. Her swan pecked at her, wanting her to go back. It didn't like Cam's presence or the possessive way he put a hand on her. "Wait," she said, just as they were about to go back inside.

"What's wrong?"

"Uh ... Sarah loves the cookies from the cafe," she said. "She'll be disappointed that we went there for lunch and I didn't get her any."

"Oh, we can—"

"No!" She waved her hands at him. "I mean ... you go ahead and go back to work. I'll grab some cookies. Bye, Cam! And thanks again." She rushed back toward the cafe, her heart pounding in her chest. What was Anders doing here, anyway? South Blackstone was out of his way. Main Street would have been closer to his place. There was something wrong. *Something happened*. She could feel it.

She skidded to a halt outside the cafe, but there was no sign of him, not even when she peeked inside. Her stomach sank. Why, she didn't know. Of all the times to run into him, it *had* to be today. Feeling defeated, she turned, but then bumped into someone. "Oomph!"

A pair of hands steadied her. When her swan flapped its wings excitedly, she knew who it was. "Anders," she breathed.

He dropped his hands to his sides. "Darcey." His jaw hardened.

Why did she even come back here, looking for him? "Um, did you get something to eat yet?" *God, that sounded lame.*

"I've lost my appetite."

His tone made her flinch. "Cam and I ... we were just having lunch," she blurted out. "As friends."

His golden eyes hardened. "You're free to do what you want, Darce. And eat lunch with whomever you want."

Her chest tightened as the air rushed out of her lungs. "Anders, don't be—"

"I should go." Shoving his hands into his jeans pockets, he turned around, shoulders hunching over as he walked away.

Her swan urged her to go to him, to tell him that the other male didn't mean anything to her. But she couldn't move. She could only watch his retreating figure as it grew smaller and farther away. Bile rose up in her throat, and she rushed into the cafe and made a beeline for their bathroom.

As she cleaned herself up in the sink, she took a deep breath. Maybe Anders was having an off day. Things would be fine between them and go back to normal—whatever normal was.

But later that night, she waited, keeping one ear open for the sound of the sliding glass door opening.

It never came. He never came. Nor did he come the next night.

As she changed from her lacey teddy to her comfy pajamas, she told herself this was for the best. Her swan, though, trilled sadly. *Don't you start*, she chided.

It was bound to end; whatever this thing was they were doing. She always knew that. There was no way it was going to last. Better now before either of them got really hurt. As far as she could tell, they hadn't bonded yet. When she asked Sarah about the bonding process, all she said that she would definitely know it if it happened.

Whatever it was she was feeling would pass, she told herself. It had to.

———

Darcey woke up a few days later feeling so miserable that Sarah had to march her back to bed. "You're staying home," she had ordered this morning. "And that's final."

Frankly, she didn't have the strength to fight her sister. The last few days had been draining, to say the least. It had been a week since the last time she'd seen Anders, and there was still no word from him. Not that she expected anything, but he didn't even text or call. What would he say? "Have a nice life?"

Ugh.

As a wave of nausea passed over her, she managed to haul herself up out of bed, and once again found herself tossing her cookies into the toilet. When she got to the sink, she looked up at the mirror and groaned at the sight that greeted her. Gaunt skin, dark circles under her eyes, hair limp. *God, I look terrible.* No wonder Sarah forced her to stay home.

She reached for her toothbrush and toothpaste, but found the tube empty. Opening her medicine cabinet, she reached for the new tube of toothpaste when something caught her eye.

Oh.

Oh no.

Sitting on the top shelf was an unopened box of tampons.

The sight of it made her go back to the toilet and vomit up whatever was left in her stomach. When she hauled herself up to the counter, she looked at herself in the mirror again.

"How could this happen?" she said aloud to her reflection.

Well, of course she knew *how*. But she was so religious about taking her birth control pills and hadn't skipped a day. Even made sure her prescription didn't lapse, not even when she moved here. The doctor at the Blackstone Women's Clinic assured her that it would be no problem to move her prescription here and that they would even give her a newer one made just for shifters. "Damn it!" She was going to give that doctor a piece of her mind.

Maybe she wasn't ... that. Oh God, she couldn't even say it. Maybe it was something she ate. A persistent bug. One that only affected shifters or swans like her. *I need to get a test.* She'd call the clinic right away as a blood test would be more accurate. And frankly, with her luck, she'd probably run into someone she knew at the drug store if she tried one of those home test kits.

Luckily, the clinic had an opening for that afternoon. She sat in the examination room, biting her lips and swinging her legs as she waited for the doctor to come in with her results. When the door did finally open, she thought she would expire from all the nervous energy building inside her.

"Miss Wednesday," Dr. Khan said as she entered the room. "Good afternoon. How are you feeling?"

"Fine. Can you tell me the results?" she snapped, but then added. "Please."

Dr. Khan peered down at the clipboard in her hand. "Congratulations. You're pregnant."

The world stopped spinning, and blood roared in Darcey's ears loudly, blocking out any sound.

"Miss Wednesday? Darcey?" Dr. Khan asked, concern marring her face. "Are you feeling ill? Do you need to go to the bathroom?"

She took a deep breath. "I'm ... all right. Just ..." Shocked didn't even begin to describe how she felt. "B-b-but how? I don't understand, Doctor. You said everything would be fine when I got my new pills."

"I did, but didn't you read the pamphlet I gave you along with the new prescription?"

"Uh ... I skimmed through it."

The doctor *tsked*. "When switching to a new brand of birth control, you need to wait a month before having unprotected sex. Plus, you know it's not one hundred percent effective. Nothing is, except for abstinence."

Right. "Uh, I'm sorry, Doctor, I didn't mean to go off on you. I just ... I wasn't expecting ..." Right now, the last thing she was expecting was *to be* expecting.

"It's quite early, Darcey." Dr. Khan put the clipboard down and slipped her glasses off. "You do have ... options. You don't have to keep it if you don't want to."

Her swan flapped its wings violently and pecked at her, wanting to come out and gouge the doctor's eyes out for suggesting such a thing. "I ..."

"You don't have to decide now," Dr. Khan add quickly. "Either way, let me know. I assure you; we will take good care of you here."

"I ... thank you so much." She burst into tears. "Oh God, I'm sorry."

The doctor smiled at her sympathetically. "It's all right. This is all normal, Darcey. It's your hormones." She cleared her throat. "Did you need anything else? Or have any questions?" Darcey shook her head. "I'll give you a few minutes, then.

When you're ready, just go to the receptionist, and I'll leave a packet of information for you."

"Th-thank you, Doctor."

A fresh wave of tears overcame her as soon as the door closed. *Pregnant.* She was pregnant. Lord. A baby. *Anders's* baby.

She buried her face in her hands and let out a groan. *What am I going to do?* God, she'd been so careful all these years! When she had been with other men, she made sure they wore a condom, but with Anders ... she just lost her head. They didn't use one that first time, and since she was on birth control and they had already done it, it seemed silly to ask him, plus shifters didn't get STDs. How was she going to tell Sarah and Adam? And Anders ...

The room suddenly felt tiny, like the walls were closing in on her. *Air, I need air.* She rushed out of the room and straight out of the clinic. Her hands were shaking as she got into her car. Placing her hands on the wheel, she took deep breaths. As soon as she felt calm enough, she started the engine and pulled out of the parking lot.

Without any destination in mind, she just drove. She kept on driving, because at least she had to concentrate on that, and she didn't have to think about anything else. Finally, she ended up at Lucas Lennox Park. She'd come here once with Adam, Sarah, and Daniel when they had some kind of annual celebration for the founder of the town.

Back in the summer, the park had been lush and green and full of life. Now, in the autumn, the trees burst with colors of fall—reds, bright oranges, and browns. The leaves were already falling, the wind picking them up and whipping them by. Darcey kept walking and walking until she came upon a park bench that had a breathtaking view of the Blackstone mountains. Up there, too, the leaves had turned. Backing up, she sat on the bench, mesmerized by the sight. Her heart ached, looking up at those mountains, wondering where Anders was, the tears building up in her eyes again.

"Are you all right?"

She started at the voice. Whipping her head to the side, she realized someone else was sitting beside her on the bench. It was a woman, probably a couple of years older than her. She was wearing baggy sweats, and her coppery red hair was pulled back into a ponytail.

"Um, yeah, I guess," she said, wiping the tears with the back of her hand. "Sorry, was I disturbing you?" She nodded at the woman's lap, where a sketchbook and a set of colored pencils lay.

The redhead sighed. "No, not at all. Are you sure you're okay?"

"Yeah. I just found out ... some news."

The woman looked up at the mountains. "Beautiful, aren't they?"

"Yeah. They are."

They sat together in silence, both of them staring up at the mountains. Moments passed. Or hours maybe. The light was waning, the setting sun setting the mountains ablaze in a glorious display of reds and oranges.

"Are you an artist?" Darcey asked, breaking the silence.

The redhead hummed noncommittally.

"Do you come here often? To draw the mountains?"

She shook her head. "No, I don't draw landscapes."

"What are you doing, then?"

Her pretty pale blue eyes glazed over and she turned back to the mountains. "Trying to find color."

"Color?" What was she talking about? There was so much color around them. As she was about to ask the other woman what she meant, Darcey noticed the heartbreaking expression on her face. "Miss? What's wrong?"

"I have to go." The redhead shot to her feet.

"Wait, I—"

She dashed off without another word, so quick in fact, that she was a mere blur to Darcey's eyes. *Huh.* Of course she was a shifter.

Turning back to the view of the mountains, her mind went back to her current predicament, her hand instinctively going down to her belly. A little cygnet was growing inside her at this very moment. Or a tiger cub. Her swan flapped its wings gleefully, eager at the idea of having a young to nurture.

How could she even think of not keeping it? She wondered if her own mother had had to make that decision. She would probably never find out about the circumstances surrounding her own birth, but she now knew what her mother might have felt and the decisions she had to face. It couldn't have been easy, and she was more convinced now that the circumstances had to have been dire for her to give up her baby.

But I was loved. As sure as she knew she loved this baby with all her heart, her own mother loved her enough to give her life. If Darcey didn't have the means to raise a child, she too would have left it with caring people.

But she was going to keep this baby.

Anders.

He would have to know. Her stomach churned at the thought of telling him, but somehow, he had to know. Even if he didn't want to raise the child, she couldn't keep it from him. They would work something out, and if he didn't want to be a father, then she would take care of the baby by herself. She would raise it and love it and make sure it knew it was loved every day of its life.

Chapter 13

The tiger stalked through the woods silently, its ears rotating as it listened for signs of intruders on its territory. There was nothing—not even the sounds of birds chirping or small animals burrowing anywhere within the vicinity. Only the sound of rain as it began to fall, pelting the dried leaves. It let out a snort and continued on roaming the area, body ready to spring at any moment.

Time to go, Anders told his tiger.

It chuffed at him and continued on.

Fine, he said disinterestedly. *Five more minutes.*

It wasn't a big deal, really. At least in this form, he didn't have to take control. He could just let his tiger roam and run and pounce all it wanted. *Maybe I should just stay like this.* Life would be simpler, and he wouldn't have to think of the outside world. Of his stupid job, stupid coworkers. Damon had been on a rampage the last couple of days, and Anders was his favorite target. Seems he couldn't do anything right, and the chief chewed him out every chance he got. *Maybe things weren't so peachy at home.* Not that he was surprised.

Mates were just trouble.

That thought brought him back to the last time he'd seen Darcey. *Fucking Cam*. That motherfucking piece of shit. Had they been seeing each other all this time? He thought for sure the other male had backed away. Seeing them walking and laughing together—him touching her—had been enough to send his already bad mood into the stratosphere. He knew he shouldn't have let that confrontation with Christopher get to him. Shouldn't have let his emotions drive him to seek comfort from her.

Well, if Cam wanted her that badly, he could have her.

His tiger growled in rage and showed his displeasure by pouncing on the nearest tree and ripping up the bark with its claws.

It made him feel better, especially when he imagined the bark was that snooty bastard's face.

Finally, the tiger seemed appeased and backed off from the shredded tree. By now, it really was getting too late, and he would miss his shift if he didn't head back now. He directed his tiger back to his trailer and started the change. Once fully back in human form, he hopped into the damp clothes he'd discarded and rounded to the front porch.

The sight of an unfamiliar red Mercedes in his driveway made him stop. Who the fuck owned this douche mobile?

"Took you long enough."

Ice froze in his veins at the sound of the feminine voice. His tiger growled, making his chest rattle. "What are you doing here, Felicia?" he asked as he hopped up to his porch.

Felicia stood there, umbrella in one hand, hair perfectly coiffed, dressed in an expensive-looking skirt suit, and her other perfectly manicured hand holding a slim cigarette. Golden eyes narrowed at him. "What did you tell him?"

"Tell who?"

"I don't have time for your games." She took a drag of her

cigarette, flicked it at her feet, and crushed it under her red-bottomed stiletto heel. "Christopher. He came to see you a couple of days ago." Placing her hands on her hips, she blocked him from his door. "What did you say to him?"

"Nothing," he spat. "Absolutely nothing."

"Then why is he asking all these questions about you? Why does he want to know who you are?"

"I don't know, okay? Leave me alone, I'm going to be late for work." He attempted to sidestep her, but she blocked him.

"You will *not* talk to my son," she hissed. "Or any of *my* children."

He pretended the stabbing ache in his chest didn't exist. "Whatever. Now—"

"You will not ruin my family," she added. "I won't let you."

"That's what you said the last time, Felicia," he shot back. "It's been over twenty years, try something different."

"I'm warning you. Don't come near us or—"

"*Or what?*" he roared, gripping her arms. Blood drained from her face. "What are you gonna do, huh? Abandon me again on my birthday? Not show up to the hospital when Dad was asking for you when his liver was failing? Or at his funeral? Cuz you already did all those things, so you don't have much left to threaten me with." His fingers dug into her flesh, and his tiger urged him to make her bleed.

Tears sprang in her eyes. "Anders—"

He shoved her away. "Leave. And never come back," he warned before yanking the door open and stomped inside his trailer. He slammed the door so hard, the walls shook.

When he heard the Mercedes's engine roar as it pulled away, he let out a growl. "Fuck!" He kicked at the couch. "Fuck. Fuck." Plopping down on an armchair, he buried his face in his hands. *I have to get out of here.* Fuck this shift. Fuck Damon.

Fuck Felicia. And fuck this shit. He was going to forget about his problems, just for one night.

Grabbing his jacket, he stormed out to his truck. The tires screeched as he backed out, and he drove like a madman. When he reached The Den, he parked and marched inside, heading straight for the bar.

"Whiskey, double-shot," he barked at Tim.

The bartender raised a bushy brow at him. "Excuse me?"

"You heard me, Grimes."

Tim said nothing, but took out a glass and poured some amber liquid into a glass. Anders reached for the whiskey, but the bartender's hand remained around the glass. "It's been a long time, son. Are you sure you want this?" Tim had known full well what Kevin Stevens had been like when he was still alive. Probably cut him off more times than he did his own hair.

He lifted his head and glared at him. "I'm sure." Slamming a couple of bills on the table, he grabbed the whiskey and moved to the far end.

Hunching over the glass, he stared into the depths of the amber liquid. *Just one sip.* It wouldn't even affect him. God knows he'd stayed away from alcohol long enough. One sip wouldn't turn him into his father. Or Felicia. He'd made damn well sure of that.

The sound of laughter made him whip his head around. There was a group of girls at the pool table, laughing and giggling as they played. One of them, a pretty blonde in a low-cut shirt caught his gaze. She winked at him and gave him that look he recognized so well.

Maybe he could finally put all those pickup lines and smooth moves he practiced all these years to good use. God knows, if Darcey could do it, so could he. He was about to get up from his stool when a hand landed on his shoulder and sat him back down.

"Fancy meeting you here," came the gruff, familiar voice.

Fucking Christ. He stared daggers at the taller man. "Krieger," he acknowledged. "Yeah, what a coincidence. Are you stalking me?" He tsked. "People are gonna start to talk." He brushed off Krieger's meaty hand. "If you excuse me—"

"That"—he nodded toward the girls at the pool table—"is not going to help."

"Mind your own business, Sarge." His tone was calm, but he was reaching his breaking point. Though Krieger was larger, Anders knew he could lay him on his back in two seconds flat and hit him in all his sensitive places.

"Damon's concerned about you. You know, he thinks you're one of the best rangers we have."

He huffed and crossed his arms over his chest.

"But he noticed you've been getting sloppy this last week. I said I'd watch out for you."

"Well, thank you very fucking much, guardian angel. But I don't need your help." He reached for the glass of whiskey.

"That's not going to solve anything either. You know that."

"Yeah, well it sure won't fucking hurt." He lifted the glass to his mouth. *One sip.* But his lips had barely touched the glass when he saw something out of the corner of his eye. Or rather, someone who had entered The Den, head swinging around as if looking for someone.

His tiger immediately stood at attention, its ears perking up as it mewled longingly. Darcey looked like an angel wearing a white sweater, matching leggings, and brown boots.

What the hell is she doing here?

He watched as she continued to glance around the room, craning her neck, stopping only when her eyes landed on him. Her mouth parted, and she straightened her shoulders and marched up to him.

"I'm gonna head to the john," Krieger said.

Before he could protest, the bear shifter was gone, and Darcey was fast approaching. *Fuck.* He placed the glass back on the bar and wrapped his fingers around it, his body going rigid as she drew nearer.

"I've been looking all over for you," she said softly, letting out a shiver. "I called the community center. They said you haven't showed up to teach this week." Her blonde hair was damp and matted to her head, and he stifled the urge to brush her locks from her face and take her into his arms to warm her.

"Been busy." He swirled the liquid in the glass, staring down at it.

"I was going to head up to your HQ, but I called first. Daniel said you weren't there either. And that you didn't even bother to tell them you weren't showing up today."

He whipped his head toward her. "What do you want, Darcey?"

To her credit, she didn't flinch. Though she looked awfully pale and nervous. "I-I wanted to talk."

"About what?"

"Us."

He snorted. "Us? What about you and Cam?"

"Oh, for God's sake! He's just a friend. Friends can eat lunch together."

"Then why didn't you tell me?" he snarled. "All this time ... have you been seeing him for lunch and then having me for dessert?"

Her face twisted in outrage. "How dare you!"

"I don't know what you want from me, Darcey." He lifted the glass once again and sniffed at the whiskey.

"Tell me it wasn't just sex."

Her words hit their mark, straight at his heart. He clenched his jaw.

"Tell me there was more to it." Her voice dropped a decibel. "That *I* meant something. As your mate."

That last word pushed him over the edge. "I told you, I'm not what you think I am. You think I'm some kind of Prince Charming? A good guy? A bad boy that can be redeemed?" He sneered. "Get this through your head, Darcey: I'm the asshole piece of shit everyone says I am. There are no layers here, no soft underbelly. I told you I don't do the mate thing. Why don't you go home? There's no place for you in my life."

If it were possible, her face turned even whiter. "Bastard." Her nostrils flared.

"Yeah, you called it." He raised the glass to her. "Congratu-fucking-lations."

Her lips pressed tightly as she huffed through her nose. "She really messed you up this bad? She walked out on you years ago, but you're still letting her live rent-free in your head?" Tears pooled at her eyes, and he fought the urge to brush them away. "This is what you want? Fine. I'll leave, then. You'll never have to see me again." Turning on her heel, she marched away from him.

All he could do was stare at her retreating figure. He tried to move, but he was paralyzed. His gut wrenched so bad, he thought he would throw up. His hand shook, and the glass slipped from his fingers, crashing on the floor loudly as it shattered into a million pieces, the whiskey splattering all over his work boots. One thought rang in his head.

She was right.

All these years, he'd been pushing people away because he didn't want anyone too close. Not because he didn't want to ruin them, but because he didn't want to have his heart stomped on all over again. And he fought the mating bond so hard because the last thing he wanted was to be like Felicia. It was his last *fuck you* to his egg donor, to reject her and everything in his

DNA that came from her. Only, he ended up hurting himself and his mate.

Darcey!

"Shit!" Shaking off the broken glass and whiskey from his boots, he made his way to the door.

"Anders!"

He stopped at the sound of the Krieger's voice. "I have to go," he said. "Er, sorry, man. Tell Damon he can punish me tomorrow. I'll even do trash duty for a month. But I have to go *now*." Not bothering to wait for the other man to respond, he dashed out the door. Where was—there! He spotted her, white-blonde hair and all white outfit, walking toward her car, only a couple of feet away.

"Darcey!" he shouted, but she didn't seem to hear him. "Darcey! I—"

The screeching of tires drowned out his voice. A dark blue Bentley limo pulled up beside Darcey, and a burly man came out.

Anders watched in horror as he seized Darcey by the arm. She screamed and tried to escape from his grip, but it was no use, and he pushed her into the vehicle.

Rage burned through him and his tiger. He let out a savage roar and bounded forward, running into the car head-on. He held his ground, growling and raising his hands as the vehicle approached. He would not let them leave, not with his *mate*. As the car drew nearer, he prepared himself, his tiger ready to pounce. But the impact never came as he was tackled to the ground.

"No!" He clawed at his attacker. "Let me go!"

"Anders. Anders!" Krieger's voice cut through his rage. "It's me."

"What the fuck, man!" He disentangled himself from the bear shifter. "They took her, Goddammit! Took my *mate*!"

"And how would getting flattened by that car have helped?" Krieger snorted. "Use your fucking head."

"I need to go after them." He shot up to his feet and marched toward his pickup.

Krieger let out a grunt. "I'm going with you."

"Whatever. Just don't get in my way." He was seeing red, and his tiger seethed with rage, its tail whipping back and forth. *I'm going to fucking murder those sons of bitches for taking what's mine.*

Chapter 14

What in the world was going on?

One minute, she was walking out of The Den, her body numb from her confrontation with Anders and then the next, a thug grabbed her and tossed her into the back of a luxurious limousine.

"Oomph!" Her butt hit the leather seats with a soft thud. "What the—" When she attempted to get up, two hands held her down. "What's going on?" The man who picked her up sat beside her, holding down her wrists. She tried to pull her hands away, but they were too strong. Her own swan flapped its wings and let out a hiss. *Shifters.* A familiar feeling washed over her. Not just any kind of shifter.

"Hello, Ms. Wednesday."

The voice made her freeze. Shaking her hair from her face, she lifted her head. A man sat across from her, looking calm and collected.

Her nose wrinkled. "Who—" she gasped. It was the man in the pinstripe suit she ran into at Rosie's.

His mouth spread into a smile that didn't reach his eyes. "I see you remember me."

"Who are you?" She already knew *what* he was. A swan, like her. "What do you want with me?"

"Uncanny. You look even more like her, the more I look at you." His light blue eyes turned vacant, as if lost. "So lovely."

What the heck was he talking about? "W-who?"

"Your mother."

It was as if a cannonball hit her in the chest. "My m-mother? You knew her?"

"Yes, I knew that bitch whore, well." The dullness in his eyes disappeared, only to be replaced with a raging blue fire. "You're practically a carbon copy of her. Elizabeth was a one of a kind beauty. I swore I would have her the moment I saw her, so I did. And with her as my mate, I was able to take control of my bevy from my old Alpha."

Elizabeth. Her mother. She recalled Marsh's words from the last time they spoke. This must be his Alpha. *Cassius.* She gasped. "Are you my—"

"Father?" Cassius finished. "No, my dear. I'm not. That honor belongs to that bastard Jack Kelly. I welcomed him and his brother into my home, and what does he do? Screw my wife and get her pregnant!"

A cold chill passed over her. "I don't understand ... I thought ... she's your mate! Why would she betray you?"

His nostrils flared, and his lips pursed together.

"Wait ..." Realization struck her. "She's not ... you weren't really mates were you?"

"Smart girl," he sneered. "Too bad your mother wasn't as wise. She was ambitious, though. She and I had an understanding—pretend to be mates so I can be Alpha, and in turn, elevate her status in the bevy. We ruled peacefully for five years. But all that changed when Jack Kelly walked in the door. He and his brother came to America to connect and make alliances with other swan bevies. He was handsome and charming, but I didn't pay any mind to him. Little did I know, he and Elizabeth were screwing each other behind my back. Kelly and his brother didn't stay long, leaving after a week.

"A few months later, she leaves me a note to tell me she's running away to be with the father of her child. I couldn't just let her go. It would expose my lie to the bevy. So, I tracked her down. She had me running around for months—I even thought she'd made it to Australia. But, no, she'd been hiding out in Nevada. Eventually I caught up with her. By that time, she was ready to pop you out." He gritted his teeth. "I let her give birth in a tiny town outside Lund. But she escaped again with the baby. Days passed, and we found her in a hospital in Summerlin by herself. She said the baby had died, and she buried it in the desert. She came home with me after that and promised she'd never reveal the true nature of our mating if I spared her life."

"But she died anyway," Darcey finished. "Of a broken heart, being separated from her *real* mate." Cassius didn't say anything, but he didn't have to. A single tear ran down her cheek. "H-how can you be sure you didn't get her pregnant? That this—this Jack Kelly is my biological father and not you?"

"I couldn't, not at first," he said. "When I saw your billboard, I had to make sure you were one of us and that you weren't just a doppelganger. Marcellus"—he nodded to the man on her right—"came to your store to confirm that you were a shifter."

She glared up at the goon. "Asshole!" But the man didn't even flinch.

Cassius laughed. "No need to be so crass, my dear. Marcellus is very loyal to me, and very, very quiet. A literal mute swan. Speaking of which, you wanted to know how I'm sure you're not mine? Well, it was your dear friend, Dr. Marsh."

"Alfie?"

"He came to me, of course, to ask about our visitors from

Down Under. And to tell me that he had found a lone black swan living in Blackstone. I ordered him never to speak about you to anyone or even go near you or I would exile him. But I just had to see you for myself."

That's why Marsh was so scared of her. And why Cassius bumped into her at Rosie's. He was probably the one who followed her to her car that evening, too, when she was spooked. "What are you ... what are you going to do with me?"

His gaze turned frosty. "Your existence is a threat to my rule."

Her heart leapt to her throat. "No!" Her swan, too, cried out in protest, wings flapping furiously. Instinctively, her hand went to her belly. *My baby.* She couldn't let them harm her or her unborn child. Anders may not want the baby, but she did. This child was wanted and loved. She would do anything to protect it.

"It'll be quick," Cassius promised her. "At least I can guarantee you that. No slow degradation over the years."

No! She couldn't let him kill her. She would fight with all her might.

"Boss!" The driver called from the front seat. "I think we're being followed."

"What?" Cassius looked behind him. "Who the hell is it? Police?"

"I don't see any lights or hear sirens," the other goon said. "Looks like a pickup truck."

Pickup truck? Hope stirred in her. But surely many people drove pickup trucks here, right?

"Lose them, you idiot!" Cassius screamed. The limo sped up, its engines roaring as it tried to outrun their pursuer.

Who could it be? When she tried to look behind her, Marcellus pulled her back down, and she cried out as pain shot up her arm.

Something caught her eye up ahead. It was as if time slowed down as something red flashed on the road. The driver must have seen it, too. The vehicle slowed as the driver engaged the brakes, but a loud thud indicated that they hit whatever it was.

The slippery conditions made them skid off the road and spin in circles. None of them were wearing their seatbelts, so she and Marcellus tumbled forward—her into the empty seat beside Cassius, and the burly goon into his employer. A loud crash indicated they must have hit something, the impact slamming her against the door.

"What the hell?" Cassius screamed furiously as Marcellus scrambled to get off him. "Get us out of here!" he barked at the driver. But the man didn't answer. "Goddammit! Marcellus, get up there and—"

A loud thud interrupted him as something heavy smashed against the side of the vehicle.

"What the—"

Glass shattered as a large paw broke through the window, pulling the entire door off.

"Goddammit!" Cassius exclaimed as one of the largest creatures she'd ever seen—a humongous bear with thick brown fur—poked its head in and roared at them, baring its teeth.

"Get him!" Cassius ordered Marcellus.

The burly goon lunged forward, tangling with the bear and tackling it to the ground. *Why would he do that?* In human or swan form, he wouldn't have had a chance against the bear.

When Cassius grabbed her arm and pulled her out the other door, she realized why. He was just distracting the bear so his boss could finish her off.

"No!" She struggled as hard as she could, digging her heels into the wet earth. However, when she heard the cock of a gun and felt something hard press against her side, she went still.

"Come now, Ms. Wednesday," he sneered. "My need for

you to die outweighs your desire to live. I have much more to lose."

Her swan hissed at him, its wings flapping madly. "Please!" she cried. "Don't." She wrapped her arms around her belly. "I'm—"

He shoved her against a tree and wrapped his hand around her neck. "You—"

The orange and black blur came at them so fast; she couldn't tell what it was. Only that it was very big and had large claws that came down on Cassius. The swan Alpha screamed in pain and doubled over, dropping to his knees.

When Darcey lifted her head, a full-grown Siberian tiger stood over the Alpha and let out a roar.

Anders! Darcey couldn't believe it, but she knew it was him, even though she'd never seen his tiger. Familiar golden eyes bore into her.

Slowly, he began to change. Limbs growing shorter and fur receding into skin. Soon, Anders stood there, chest heaving, those honey eyes never leaving her.

"Darcey," he whispered hoarsely as he moved toward her.

She attempted to stand, but her knees wobbled, sending her forward. He was in front of her in a nanosecond, lifting her up into his arms. "A-Anders. He-he tried to—"

"Shh ... beautiful." He pressed a kiss to her forehead. "You're safe." Glaring down at the Alpha, he spat, "He won't be going anywhere."

When she tried to see what he had done to Cassius, he whirled her around, then started to walk away. "I've called P.D. They should be on their way. They'll take care of him."

She felt faint, and her stomach churned. An ice-cold feeling washed over her, and her swan beat its wings in a panicked rhythm. "Anders. *Anders.* Put me down."

"In a second." He continued walking, out into the road, past the smashed Bentley. A chill passed over her again as she saw Marcellus's prone body. "Anders, there's a bear loose—"

"I know," he said. "He's a friend. C'mon, there he is." He frowned. "What the heck—"

Turning to where Anders was looking, she saw a huge, naked man kneeling on the side of the road, clutching something. No, not something. *Someone.*

"Geez! Krieger, what are you—" Anders froze.

With him distracted, Darcey managed to untangle herself from Anders's arms. Her feet touched the ground with an unsteady gait, so she held onto him. "What's going—" She gasped, her hand going to her mouth.

The man—Krieger—held the figure of a frail, naked woman, her long, coppery locks spilling over his arms like a bloody waterfall.

"No!" He let out an anguished cry and clutched the woman to him. "Please. No." Sobbing, he buried his face in her hair. "Don't leave me. I'm sorry. I'm sorry I couldn't be better."

"Anders? What's—" She dug her fingers into his arm as sharp, shooting pain struck her in the abdomen.

"Darcey?" He caught her before she collapsed. "What's wrong? Are you hurt?"

Looking down between her legs, she saw it—the red seeping through her white leggings and down her thighs. "No ..." she managed to whisper before the world turned black.

Chapter 15

Anders didn't know how much time had passed. Hell, he couldn't even recall how he got here in the sterile, antiseptic-smelling waiting room of Blackstone Hospital. When he closed his eyes, the only thing he could see was red. All that blood. Darcey.

"Here, man, have some of this."

Lifting his head, he nodded gratefully at Daniel, who offered him a paper cup. "Thanks." He took a sip of what he assumed was coffee, but it was hard to tell. It tasted like ashes on his tongue.

"Do you want to talk about what happened?"

"I ..." His chest tightened. All he could remember was him and Krieger chasing down the limo, then seeing it crash. Krieger got to the limo first and tore it open, but he saw another man drag Darcey out. He recalled shifting and the taste of blood and flesh in his mouth. Then holding Darcey.

The paramedics arrived just in time. Thankfully, Krieger had been thinking clearly and immediately got on the phone with P.D., keeping them updated on their whereabouts as they chased Darcey's kidnappers. After that ... everything was a blur.

Krieger. Where was he? And that woman on the road. *Who* was she?

"Any news yet?" Daniel asked as Sarah approached them.

She shook her head. "No, I just came from the nurses' station." Sitting down beside Anders, she placed a hand on his shoulder. "Thank you. Thank you for going after her."

His stomach churned, and he remained silent. What could he say? Darcey had run from him. No, he pushed her away, and now there was a possibility she could die, and she would never know how much she meant to him.

"Are you the family of Ms. Darcey Wednesday?"

All three of them shot to their feet. "How is she?" Anders said.

The doctor narrowed his eyes. "Which one of you is her family?"

"I'm her sister," Sarah said.

"And her brother-in-law," Daniel added.

"Come with me." The doctor gestured for them to follow him. But when Anders followed, he put a hand up. "And you, sir? Are you family?"

"It's all right," Sarah said, giving him a weak smile. "He can come."

"Fine, but you can't stay too long, and you must let her rest." They followed the doctor down the hall, and entered the second room on the right. Filing in, they made a beeline for the lone bed where Darcey lay, dressed in a drab hospital gown, her arm hooked up to an IV drip.

The sight of her, looking so frail, made Anders panic. His tiger, too, didn't like it. He rushed toward her. "Darcey. Oh God."

When her gaze landed on him, she went even paler. "What are you doing here?"

"Darcey, please—"

"I don't want him here," she cried, pleading to the doctor. "You said family only. Please, tell him to leave."

Anders felt his gut clench. "Darcey, I'm sorry, for what I said—"

"No!" She grabbed at Sarah, who had rushed to her other side. "Tell him to go! I don't want to see him!"

"But, Darcey, he saved you," Sarah reasoned. "And he's your mate, don't you want—"

"Get out!" she screamed at him. "Get out. Get out!"

The words struck him like a knife to the chest and made it hard to breathe. His tiger mewled at her rejection of them.

"Ms. Wednesday, please," the doctor said. "I warned you, you can only see your family if you stay calm. We can't have you stressed, not with you almost losing the baby."

Blood drained from Darcey's face, and she let out a sob.

"Baby?" Anders felt like he'd been hit by a cannonball in the gut. "You're pregnant?"

"Pregnant?" Sarah repeated. Slowly, her head turned toward him, her nostrils flaring. "Leave."

"But I—"

"She doesn't want you here." She clutched Darcey to her chest. "Daniel, please!"

Daniel stepped forward, blocking him from advancing. "Let's go."

"I can't—"

"I said, let's *go.*" His silvery blue eyes glowed with the power of his animal. An arm came up to his shoulder and pushed him toward the door as Darcey's sobs filled the room.

Powerless, he allowed Daniel to lead him out. "Daniel, please—"

"I warned you," Daniel snarled. "If you didn't have plans to claim her, just leave her alone. You couldn't even do that, could you, you selfish bastard!"

"She's having my baby!" *Oh God. Darcey. A baby.* And they'd almost lost it. "Please, man, just let me talk to her alone."

"No! I won't have you upsetting her again."

"Christ!" He raked his hands through his hair. What was he going to do? "Daniel, please. What if it was you? And what if it was Sarah in there? With *your* baby?"

Daniel's face hardened. "You can't say anything to change my mind. You don't deserve her."

"Please ... Dan ..." He swallowed the lump in his throat. "You're right, I don't. Not since the moment I was born did I deserve anything or anyone like her. All I do is ruin everything I touch. Anyone I come in contact with. Starting with my own mother."

And then it all spilled out. He confessed to Daniel every single detail of his wretched life, from the moment his mother walked out on him on his birthday, to that afternoon when Felicia came to see him and he eventually pushed Darcey away. "... I swear, until the doctor said something, I had no idea she was pregnant. I was doing it for her." He gripped Daniel's arm. "I thought ... I thought it was for the best she stayed away from me. I wanted her, but I'm no good for her."

Daniel scrubbed a hand down his face. "Anders ... man ... I don't know what to say."

"I ... I love her," he choked out. "And I can't live without her." His tiger roared in pain, and his gut twisted. "Just ... five minutes.

The bear shifter held up his hands. "I'm sorry, it's not up to me. If Darcey doesn't want to see you, I can't make her."

"I'll wait. I don't care how long, I'll wait."

Daniel looked back at the door and then at him. "I hope you're willing to wait a while. Look," he placed a hand on his shoulder. "I'll ... I'll talk to Sarah and to Darcey."

"Thanks, man." He sighed. "You're a good friend."

"Don't thank me yet." Turning on his heel, he disappeared into Darcey's room.

Anders stared at the closed door, unsure what to do. His tiger wanted him to go in there and claim their mate and their cub, but he knew he couldn't push it. Jesus Christ. *A baby*. He'd never asked Darcey about protection, and he always assumed she was safe. That's what she wanted to talk to him about at The Den. When he told her all those terrible things.

Was it any wonder that Darcey didn't want to see him? After how he treated her? He shoved his fingers into his hair. "Fuck." He really did it this time. Made her believe that he was a no-good bastard by treating her like trash. Closing his eyes, he could still picture the heartbreaking look on her face when he told her there was no place for her in his life. And when she fainted, and all that blood ... the baby nearly—

"Anders."

He spun around at Daniel's voice. "Yes?"

The expression on the other man's face told him it wasn't good news. "She needs rest. Sarah's going to stay with her. I'm gonna go home and check on Adam and come back with some stuff for Sarah. Do you need anything?"

"No."

"Why don't you go home, man?" Daniel suggested. "Get some sleep."

He shook his head. "No. I'm going to stay here."

Daniel let out a breath. "All right." Reaching over, he squeezed Anders's shoulder. "I'll see you around."

"Thanks."

Grabbing an unused chair from the nurses' station, he placed it by the door and camped outside her room.

The hours blurred by. Nurses came and went into the room. Night must have passed at some point, but he didn't sleep.

Morning came. The shift changed as a different set of nurses walked by him and made their rounds.

The sound of Darcey's door opening made his heart jump, and he shot to his feet. "Sarah." He swallowed hard. "How is she?"

The look of contempt on her face was unmistakable. "So, you're still here."

"I can't leave." He took two steps toward her. "Please. She's mine. My mate. And that child is mine."

She pointed a finger at his face. "Correction: you *were* her mate. But you gave that up when you rejected her."

"I didn't." He cursed under his breath. "I mean ... I only did that because I tried to protect her. From me."

"Really? And was getting her pregnant part of your plan?"

"You're mated," he said. "You know what it's like, and how you felt when you first met Daniel. Darcey's a shifter, so imagine that feeling tenfold. Imagine a voice, an animal inside you, telling you every single moment of the day that your mate is there, and you need to be with them."

"Don't you dare put this on her," Sarah hissed. "If it were up to me, you'd never see her again. But it's not."

"What—" He stopped short, noticing the annoyed look on her face. "She wants to see me, doesn't she?"

Sarah's nostrils flared, and she folded her arms over her chest. "Against my better judgement, yes."

Hope flared in his chest. He didn't even bother to ask permission, and instead, just barreled into the room. "Darcey!"

She wasn't in bed. Instead, she was standing by the window, looking outside.

"Darcey, what are you doing?" Panic rushed through him. "Why are you out of bed? You should be—"

"I'm fine, Anders," she said flatly. "I'm all healed. In fact, Sarah's getting all my discharge papers ready."

"Darcey, I'm sorry." He reached out to touch her, but she flinched away, so he dropped his hand to his side. "About what I said. I didn't mean any of it."

She shut her eyes and took a deep breath. "You don't have to say that."

"But—"

"Really. You know about the baby now. And ... frankly, it's a relief." Her shoulders dropped. "I was going to tell you at The Den. But now ... now you saved me the trouble."

"Saved you the trouble?" *What was she saying?*

"I wouldn't have kept the baby a secret from you," she said in a quiet voice. "I doubt I could have. But I want you to know, you don't have to do anything. We'll be fine."

"F-fine?" A throbbing pulse built up behind his eyes.

"Yeah. I'll take care of the baby. You can have visitation; I won't fight you."

"Darcey, what are you saying?"

She wrapped her arms around her belly protectively. "Or if you don't, that's fine too."

"Are you nuts? Darcey. *Darcey*, look at me." But she kept her gaze fixed toward the outside. He wanted to reach out to her, but she looked so fragile, he feared she would turn to dust if he so much as touched her arm. "Darcey ... I love you. Please. I want to be with you. Be your mate. Raise our baby together. Please tell me you feel the same way."

Her eyes shut and she didn't speak for a few seconds. As he waited on tenterhooks, the silence stretched between them until she finally spoke. "I don't know how I feel, Anders. When you said those words at The Den—"

"I didn't mean them."

"But you didn't know I was pregnant then, either," she pointed out. "I don't want you to feel obligated to be with me because of the baby. So ... I'm letting you go."

A knife-like pain sliced through his chest. It was worse than anything he'd felt before, not even on that day Felicia walked out without so much as a backward glance. "No."

"Please, Anders, just go."

"I said, *no*."

Her head whipped around, as she finally met his gaze. "What do you mean, *no*?"

"I'm not giving up. Not without a fight." *Never.* "I've made mistakes in the past, but I know one thing: you and me, that's it for me. No one, and nothing else matters. And I'm not walking out on this child."

Her brows snapped together. "I told you, you can visit all you want—"

"That's not enough, Darcey," he warned. "I want it all. I want our child, and I want you."

She gasped. "I said I don't know—."

"I've hurt you, and I'm sorry." He took a tentative step toward her. "But I'm damned well not giving up on you." Darcey would be his, there was no doubt in his mind.

Her arms folded over her chest. "I'm not going to make it easy."

That spark of emotion gave him hope. At least she wasn't indifferent to him. "Good. I don't expect you to." Every instinct in his body told him to stay. His tiger pleaded him not to leave their mate. *We have to go*, he told it. But it won't be forever.

The things he had said to her to push her away had been cruel, even if he didn't mean it. And he knew he had to make it up to her, somehow. He would face every punishment she meted out, anything she did or said, he would accept like a lash on his back. Because he deserved it. So, despite his tiger's protests, he turned and walked out of the room.

As he made his way back to the waiting area, something caught his eye—in the room opposite of Darcey's. The door was open just a crack, but it was enough for him to see inside. He crept closer, pushing the door open.

There was a woman sleeping on the bed, and some kind of machine hooked up to her. But that wasn't what caught his attention No, it was the large, hulking man in the chair next to her, head hidden by a curtain of dark hair, his humungous hand covering hers. Krieger didn't move or make a sound except for the steady rising and falling of his chest as he slept. *Huh.* Something clicked in Anders's brain.

To be a better man.

He understood the other man's words now. He wanted to be a better man. For *her.*

As he finished a silent prayer to whatever god could hear him, Anders could only hope he could be better too. For Darcey and their baby.

Chapter 16

Darcey stared after him, still reeling from shock. She didn't know how long she stood there, slack-jawed, her eyes fixed on the door. It must have been a long time, because it felt like she didn't move, not until Sarah came in.

"Darce?" Her sister cocked her head as she approached. "Are you okay?"

"I ... yeah."

"What did he say?"

She shrugged. "Can we go now?"

"Sure, Darce."

They left the room and headed straight to the exit. Daniel was already there, waiting by the car. As he opened the door of his truck for her, he gave her a sad, sympathetic smile.

The ride home was silent, and soon they reached the house. They were barely inside when Adam came rolling out of the kitchen. The look on his face—a mix of shock, relief, and joy— broke Darcey's heart, and she opened her arms to him. Sarah said they told him everything that happened, except the pregnancy part. He had insisted on coming to the hospital, but

Daniel assured him multiple times that Darcey was all right, but the doctor wanted to keep her overnight just in case.

"You're okay," he whispered as she hugged him, his face pressed into her side.

"Yeah, I'm tougher than I look." She ruffled his hair. "That's the advantage of having a sister who's a shifter." Hopefully that would reassure him. He must have been worried out of his mind —first, Sarah and Daniel had been attacked by an anti-shifter group last summer, and now Darcey was the one whose life had been threatened.

"I made breakfast," he said with a sniff. "I figured you'd be hungry."

"Breakfast sounds awesome." Though to be honest, her stomach felt queasy, but she would try to eat what she could. "Let's eat and we can talk."

After the events of the summer with Sarah and Daniel's accidental marriage, they had all vowed to be honest with each other and not keep things from Adam since he was nearly an adult. So, as they ate the pancakes and bacon Adam made, she told them about her real parents, Cassius, and what happened the previous night.

Daniel's jaw hardened. "I'll call P.D. and get an update on that guy. Last I heard, they brought him to the hospital and he's alive, but we'll make sure to put him away for good for what he did to you and your mother."

"Hold on." Adam put his fork and knife down. "If your bio dad is from a bevy in Perth and the brother of the Alpha, then that means he could still be alive, right? And that you have other family?"

With all the events of yesterday and this morning, she hadn't even thought of that. "Maybe. If he didn't die when they were separated, like my mother."

"At least we could find the rest of your bevy," Adam said. "And connect you with them."

Sarah reached over and covered her hand with hers. "Darcey, if it's true ... I'm so happy for you."

"I ..." She didn't know how to react to that. All her life, she thought she was the only one of her kind. To think that there may be others ... and they could be her relatives ... "Sarah, I told you—"

"I know, Darce. We'll always be family. But if you have a chance to get to know that part of your background and your shifter side, you should take it."

"Yeah," Adam agreed wholeheartedly. "I'll do the research. I'm sure it won't be hard to find a Jack Kelly who's a black swan shifter from Australia. Maybe you could go and visit them when we find out."

The idea both scared and excited her, and her swan let out a joyous trill. Of course, traveling may have to wait. Which reminded her of her other news. "There's something else you should know, Adam." As she looked at Daniel and Sarah, they both gave her encouraging smiles. "You're going to be an uncle."

He blinked. "A what now?"

"I'm having a baby," she said.

"Oh." He chewed on a piece of bacon thoughtfully, then swallowed. "Is it Anders's?"

Three pairs of eyes zeroed in on him. "H-how did you know?" Darcey asked.

Adam rolled his eyes. "Please. You think I haven't seen him the backyard sneaking into your room?"

Darcey felt her face flush, and she shot an apologetic look to Daniel.

"So, you guys are mates? Are you going to get married, too?" Adam scratched his chin. "Is he moving in?"

Daniel choked on his orange juice. "Er ..."

"No, Adam," she said. "It's not working out."

"What?" His lips pursed together. "But he's the father of your baby. Does he not want it? Why would he just leave you—"

"It's complicated."

"What's complicated?" He nodded at Sarah and Daniel. "They're mates, and they're together. It's supposed to be easy for you shifters, right? You just know? Doesn't he want you?"

A heavy weight pressed against her chest. "I wish I knew what to tell you, Adam." She fought the tears welling in her eyes. She didn't know what to believe. The shock of nearly losing her baby had turned her inside-out. And then there were Anders's hurtful words from the day before. *There's no place for you in my life.*

He didn't know she was pregnant before he told her all those things. And he was right: He'd always been honest with her about what he wanted and didn't want. She was the one who invited him into her bed even though he said he didn't do the mate thing. How could she be sure he wanted to stay with her because of her, and not just the baby or the shock of nearly losing it? Despite his confession of love, it was hard for her to believe him. What if he hurt her again? Frankly, her heart wouldn't be able to survive it.

The doorbell ringing knocked her out of her reverie.

"I'll get it," Daniel said, getting up from his chair.

"You do what's best for you, Darce," Sarah said. "You and the baby. You know you'll always have a place here."

Adam huffed. "If he doesn't want you, then ... then he can go eat a dick!"

"Adam!" Sarah admonished.

"C'mon, Sarah, you've thought worse about him, I bet," Adam shot back.

Daniel walked into the kitchen and looked at Darcey. "You might want to come see this."

"See what?" But her brother-in-law was already gone.

Puzzled, she got up from her chair and followed Daniel out into the hallway and to the front door. He cocked his head outside.

She gasped as she peeked out. The front lawn was filled with flowers of all kinds—roses, peonies, sunflowers, daisies, gardenias—strewn about in various arrangements.

"I gotta say, when he wants to catch your attention, he really goes all out," Daniel said.

Her swan flittered inside her enthusiastically, but she squashed it down. "They're just flowers," she said.

"Yeah, and Kilimanjaro is just a mountain," Adam said, as he rolled up next to her. "I think this means he does want you."

"He wants the baby," she pointed out. *Not me.*

"Aww, Darce, can't you give him a chance?" her brother asked.

"You're on his side?" That came out harsher than she intended. "Sorry."

"He's a good guy," Adam said. "You know that, with all the work he does at the community center and those kids. He'll be a great dad."

"Kids?" Daniel asked.

"Community center?" Sarah said at the same time.

"Yeah." Adam explained to them about meeting Anders and his work with the kids at the community center.

"I'll be damned." Daniel scratched his head.

"Are you sure that was Anders, and not his twin?" Sarah asked.

"I'm sure. Say what you want about him, but he's one of the good ones out there," Adam insisted.

Darcey sighed. Adam had only seen that side of Anders, of course. He didn't know the rest.

"Can we finish breakfast now?" the teen asked.

"All right," Sarah said. "Darce?"

"You go ahead," she said, waving them away. "I just need a moment."

As the three of them went back to the kitchen, she remained at the door, staring at the sea of flowers. They must have cost a fortune, especially in this season. With a sigh, she hopped down the stoop and bent down to pick up a vase of roses.

"Darcey."

A tingle ran up her spine, and her swan lifted its head, whistling enthusiastically. Swallowing the lump in her throat, she stood up straight.

Anders stood at the edge of the front lawn, staring up at her. He'd showered and changed, though the stubble he had grown remained. Golden eyes bore right into her, and she tensed.

"You didn't have to do this," she said.

"I know. But I wanted to."

She picked up another arrangement—a basket full of daisies. "You can't send me a whole florist shop to get what you want."

"Tell me what I have to do then." His tone was deadly serious.

She stared at him and swallowed a gulp. The look in his eyes made her stomach flip, and her swan flapped its wings at her, urging her to go to him. But she ignored her animal. "I don't know, Anders. I just ... I need time. And space."

He let out a breath. "All right." Turning on his heel, he walked back to his truck. He slipped into the driver's side, but he didn't start the engine or pull away. No, he sat there, and even from across the street, his golden gaze pinned her to the spot.

Pressing her lips tight, she forced herself to turn around and walk back into the house. *I can't do this again.* It was one thing for her to have her heart broken, but now she had to think of her baby. Her hand crept down to her stomach. From now on, she would have to think of not just herself, but the life growing inside her.

———

More deliveries came after the flowers later that day. Other gifts came too, like stuffed toy animals—including a life-sized tiger that she couldn't deny made her smile—chocolates, cakes, and even a whole four-course meal that was enough to feed ten people.

The entire time, Anders was outside, sitting patiently in his truck. He didn't approach her when she came out to receive the deliveries, but she could feel those golden honey eyes on her. Her swan pined hopelessly, but she ignored it, adding each gift to the over-flowing pile in the living room.

The next day, she insisted on going to work with Sarah, and sure enough, more flowers showed up outside the shop. At lunchtime, a delivery from *Shin Nihon* came, and in the afternoon, pastries and coffee from the cafe. When she got home after closing up, Adam was already digging into the boxes of takeout scattered across the kitchen table.

"General Tso's?" he offered cheekily. "It's your favorite."

With a grumble, she sat next to him and grabbed a box. She was starving, after all. *But this doesn't mean anything*, she told herself, even as the delicious spicy-citrusy flavor of the chicken appeased her hungry stomach.

"Aren't you going to at least talk to him?" Adam asked.

She shoved more chicken and rice into her mouth to avoid the question. It was hard to believe that Anders had somehow swayed her brother onto his side.

By the end of the week, Darcey was running out of space for all the gifts and flowers, as well as patience. "This is getting ridiculous. This has got to stop," she said as she deposited the bouquet of orchids on top of the counter next to the register.

"He sure is persistent," Sarah said. "I have to give him that at least."

"Hmph." Clamping her lips shut, Darcey turned back to checking the invoices against their POS system.

Later that evening, as she was closing up the office, she heard the door open. *No, not another delivery*, she groaned silently. "We're closed," she called out. "You can—" But it wasn't a delivery from Anders. It was Anders himself.

"Hi, Darcey."

Dressed in a shirt, tie, and suit, she almost didn't recognize him. "What are you doing here?"

"I wanted to take you out to dinner."

"Dinner?"

"Yes. On a date."

She blinked. They'd never been on an actual date before, since he didn't consider the first time at *Shin Nihon* to be a date.

"On a real date," he added, as if reading her mind. "Will you come to dinner with me?"

"You can't keep doing this," she said. "You need to stop with the gifts and deliveries."

"I will. If you go out to dinner with me."

"I—" She rubbed the bridge of her nose with her thumb and forefinger. "All right."

His face lit up. "Really?"

"Let's go before I change my mind."

"Where do you want to go?"

"It doesn't matter."

They ended up at the French restaurant a few blocks down. The food was good, and the atmosphere was romantic. Well, almost. It would have seemed like a romantic date, except that Anders barely said a word. He sat across her, looking at her somberly, like he was afraid to say anything that might upset her. So, he remained quiet, only asking her if she liked the food or if she needed more salt.

"Thanks for the meal," she said, as he paid for their check.

"You're welcome."

There was something not quite right, and she didn't know what it was. Something she couldn't quite put her finger on. He walked her to her car and said goodnight, then hopped into his own car. Of course, as she drove back, she saw him right behind her, following her all the way home. When she pulled into the driveway, he remained parked outside, not leaving until she was safely indoors.

The next day, there was still that niggling feeling. She opened the boutique since Sarah wanted to go to her usual Saturday morning yoga class. To her surprise, her sister didn't come back afterwards alone. J.D. and Anna Victoria joined her.

"Hey, ladies," she greeted. "It's been a while."

J.D. immediately enveloped her in a hug. "I'm sorry I haven't been by sooner. Work's been hell." Darcey had given Sarah permission to tell them everything that had happened.

"I'm sorry too," Anna Victoria added, chewing her lip. "Been working on a couple things."

"We just came back from visiting Dutchy," J.D. said.

"Oh my God, how is she?" Sarah had relayed to Darcey about the young woman Cassius's driver had run over. While it had made it easier for Anders and Krieger to catch up to them, Darcey felt awful that the young woman had been hurt in the process.

"She's improving everyday," J.D. said somberly.

"But she's a shifter, right?" Darcey asked. "I know getting hit by a car is worse than what I went through, but I healed up right away. What could be the matter?"

J.D. shrugged. "We don't know. The doctors don't have an

explanation as to why she's not healing as fast as she should be, either."

"What about Krieger?" Sarah asked.

J.D. and Anna Victoria looked at each other, and the mechanic spoke up first. "He's ... hanging around her."

"Do you know what happened there? With them?"

J.D. shook her head. "Not at all. No one knows."

"I think Damon knows, but he won't break Krieger's confidence," Anna Victoria added.

"But how are you feeling?" J.D. asked, glancing down at her stomach. "And ..."

"It's fine. We're fine," she said with a smile, her hand going around her stomach protectively. "Dr. Parrish said it was a good thing I'm a shifter and heal quick. If I had been human, the impact of the car crash could have ..." She choked, suddenly realizing how close she had been to losing her baby.

"Shh ... it's okay." Sarah put an arm around her.

"Say, are you guys opening a flower shop?" J.D. asked, glancing at all the bouquets and vases around the boutique.

Sarah rolled her eyes. "They're from Anders."

"All of them? You're shitting me." J.D.'s gaze narrowed at Darcey. "Is he doing the grand gesture thing?"

"Grand gesture thing?" Anna Victoria's brows furrowed.

"You know." The mechanic let out an exasperated sigh. "Like in the movies, when the guy has to prove his love to the girl by doing all these grand gestures. What else has he done?"

"We went out to dinner last night," Darcey confessed.

"Really?" Sarah looked at her incredulously.

"Yeah." She relayed to them what happened, including that weird feeling she had that there was something off with him.

"You know," Sarah began. "Daniel told me Anders is getting quite the ribbing at work."

She didn't want to ask, but she couldn't help it. "Why?"

Sarah snorted. "It turns out all that bad boy, man-whore act was just that—an act." She relayed the story of how Anders would "take home" women, but was really protecting them. "He never slept with any of them, according to Damon, who confirmed it from a reliable source."

Now that shocked her most of all. For one thing, he seemed to know what he was doing in bed, so she would have thought he was very experienced. For another—why would he want people to *think* he was a playboy without sleeping around when he could easily build that reputation by just being a man slut?

"Tits on a dog, no way!" J.D. exclaimed. "Why the hell would he want a reputation as a sleazebag?"

"He's a guy, who knows why they do things?" Anna Victoria said with a shrug.

"It doesn't matter anyway," Darcey said. But still, it bothered her.

"Look, whatever you want, we'll support you," J.D. said. "Remember what we said? No more bending over backwards to please a man? Breaking the cycle?"

"Right." The New Darcey. Had she forgotten?

The two women stayed for another twenty minutes until Anna Victoria bade them goodbye as she had another class to teach, and J.D. had to go back to work. Sarah urged her to leave the boutique in the afternoon and do something for herself or go home and rest since she didn't have to pick up Adam at school. Darcey didn't want to argue, and so she got her purse and headed out, waving to Sarah as she exited. Unfortunately, that meant she wasn't paying attention to what was in front of her, so she slammed into something solid.

"Sorry—" Her mouth clamped shut as she felt a pair of arms wrap around her. A familiar, delicious scent filled her nostrils, making her and her swan shiver excitedly.

"Hey," Anders greeted softly, his arms still around her. "Sorry, I didn't see you coming out."

"It's—it's fine." She disentangled herself from him. "Um, what are you doing here?"

"I just wanted to see if you were hungry. Thought I'd pick you up some pastries from the cafe." He glanced down at her purse. "Leaving already?"

"I opened today, so I have the rest of the afternoon off."

"Why don't we go to Rosie's?" he suggested.

"I—"

"It's been a while since I've had some of Temperance's special pies. I bet she's come up with more awesome flavors."

Her stomach gurgled loudly, and she blushed.

"Is that a yes?"

"I guess so."

Darcey told herself she was only doing this because she was hungry. She peeked over at Anders as they walked to the parking lot. What was this nagging feeling in her brain? He was just so ... different. Like this was a completely different person. Gone was the confident, pushy, and snarky man who made her laugh. He was walking on eggshells all the time around her, acting so subdued, like he was so afraid she'd disappear into thin air if he said or did anything wrong. She didn't know what to expect when he said he wasn't giving up on her. But it wasn't *this*, whatever this was.

Chapter 17

For the next week, Anders did stop sending excessive amounts of gifts, but he was always hanging around the shop during the day, ready to bring her to lunch or take her to dinner. He was polite and nice to her each time, which only made her feel awkward.

There was no mention of the baby, but he always asked how she was feeling, if she was nauseous or didn't have an appetite. Once in a while, she'd catch him glancing down at her stomach.

It was like every spare moment he had was devoted to bringing her, her favorite treats and food, or being around to help her with any errand, like going to the office supply store or dropping off deliveries at the post office. She wondered if he even had time to go to work or teach his karate classes, because he seemed to be around her all the time, following her as she went to the boutique and back home, but he never mentioned the baby, their relationship, or told her he loved her or tried to convince her that they should be together.

"It's been almost two weeks," Sarah said, nodding outside the window. Anders stood outside Silk, Lace, and Whispers, waiting for when Darcey would leave to pick up Adam. "What's going on there?"

Darcey put aside the pile of bras she was putting on hangers. "I don't know, Sarah."

"What do you guys do?" Her sister put her hands on her hips. "He's around all the time. You guys go out to dinner. I don't think he sleeps, though I've seen him dozing off in his truck when he's parked outside the house."

"I said, I don't know," she snapped. Her own harshness surprised her. "I'm sorry, Sarah. It's just …"

Sarah sat down next to her and put an arm around her. "I get it. He said some things and did things to hurt you. But you can't go on like this."

"I know."

"You're hurting him and … you're hurting yourself."

"I'm not—"

"Don't contradict me," Sarah warned. "I can see it. And it's not good for the baby when you're upset like this. Now, what's the matter?"

She took a deep, cleansing breath. "It's like … there's something not right. With the way he acts."

"What do you mean?"

"He's been so nice and polite to me. Never oversteps his boundaries. He'd bending over backwards to please me."

Sarah chuckled. "And *that* bothers you?"

"Yeah. I mean—" She rubbed her temple. "I know it's weird … but it's just not him. I thought … I thought maybe that was what I wanted. But it's not."

Sarah's brows furrowed. "So … you want him to be that man-whoring asshole he's had everyone thinking he is all this time?"

"Yes. No. I mean, I don't know." Raising her hands in

defeat, she got up and placed the hangers of bras on the display rack. "Look, it's almost time for me to get Adam."

"All right. Daniel and I are going to the movies, so I'll see you in the morning."

Darcey grabbed her keys and phone. "Bye, Sarah." As soon as she was out the door, Anders straightened his stance.

"Ready to pick up Adam?" he said.

She blew out a breath. "Yup." She didn't even try to shake him off. It didn't work. He was like a shadow.

The high school was halfway between the boutique and Daniel's house, which was why it was so convenient for her or Sarah to pick Adam up after work. He was already waiting outside chatting with some friends when she pulled up and opened the van door for him.

"He's still here?" Adam asked as he cocked his head behind him, where Anders's pickup truck had stopped.

"Yup."

Adam strapped his chair in. "Aren't you going to put him out of his misery yet? He's been groveling for two weeks now."

Looking up at the rearview mirror, she smirked at him. "And what do you know about groveling?"

"I heard chicks dig it."

"Oh yeah?" she asked. "And were there any 'chicks' you wanted to grovel to?"

Adam's face flushed "No."

"Uh-huh," she said, copying that typical, sarcastic teenage boy tone he employed when he was being smart with them. Thankfully, Adam didn't bring up Anders again. She was safe from her brother's questions and meddling. But maybe that was a mistake. Because when they pulled up to the house and he rolled out of the van, he turned his chair and rolled down the driveway.

"Anders!" he called out to the pickup truck parked across the street. "Anders!"

"What are you doing?" she asked in a panicked voice.

He rolled his eyes. "Adults," he muttered. "Hey, Anders."

Anders jogged over to them. "What is it? Do you need help? Darcey, are you okay?"

"She's fine," Adam said. "But I want pizza for dinner tonight."

"Adam!" she admonished.

"Sure thing, bud." Anders said. "I can run down to Giorgios, or Pizza Shack or—"

"No, no." Adam shook his head. "I want to order in. And I want you to join us."

"Adam—"

"Daniel said this was my home, too, and I could invite anyone over when I want to," Adam said smugly. "And I'm inviting him."

Her lips pursed. "Fine." She turned to Anders. "No anchovies. On anything."

The smile he flashed made something flutter in her chest. "Yes, ma'am."

Not bothering to wait for them, she headed inside and to her room. As she changed into her comfier clothes, she couldn't stop thinking about that smile. It reminded her of times before this whole mess. When they were just sneaking around and enjoying each other's bodies and company. It seemed so simple then—just him and her and a bed.

Padding out toward the living room, she saw Anders and Adam settled in on the couch with cans of soda.

"My friend Eun Ae told me about this cool TV show on Movieflix," Adam said as he flipped through the streaming service's selection on the giant screen TV. "She says it's got everything. Great action, dialogue, and a mind-blowing plot twist at the end."

"Really?" Darcey plopped between him and Anders on the couch. "And this Eun Ae, is she one of *those chicks*?" she teased.

Adam's face turned beet red. "No," he denied, but the way he said it made Anders throw back his head and laugh.

"Dude, you're not going to be a chickenshit around her, are ya?" Anders asked. "Because girls like a guy with confidence." He winked at Darcey.

There it was again. She couldn't help herself as she stared at him. It struck a chord in her, but of what, she didn't know.

"Just watch the show," Adam grumbled.

Darcey settled in, tucking her feet under her. As the opening credits started, she shivered, and immediately, a blanket was placed over her lap. She flashed Anders a grateful smile, her stomach doing a somersault as it hit her how gorgeous he was, with the light from the TV illuminating the planes of his face.

Halfway through the pilot episode, the pizza arrived. Anders waved her away when she tried to get up, and went to door himself. He also brought paper plates and more drinks, and distributed slices so as not to interrupt their viewing.

They continued to watch the show, but after the third episode, Adam let out a yawn. "Oh man, I should get to bed."

Darcey eyed him suspiciously. "It's Friday night, you don't have school tomorrow."

"Yeah, but I'm a growing boy, and I need my sleep. You guys can keep watching. It's an interesting show." He winked at her as he propped himself onto his wheelchair. "'Night, Darce. 'Night, Anders," he said, waving as he left the living room.

"Um, I don't have to stay," Anders said, clearing his throat. "I can go if you want."

"You don't have to go," she said quickly. "I mean, if you don't want to."

He rubbed the back of his head with the heel of his hand. "Uh, maybe one more episode?"

She grinned. "Sure."

They played the next episode, and then the next. At some point, Darcey felt her eyes get heavier, and she settled deeper into the couch. Glancing over at Anders, she saw that his eyes were closed. Her animal fluttered around in happiness, being so close to him. He looked so peaceful like this, and she couldn't help but reach over and caress his cheek.

"Darcey ..." he murmured, nuzzling at her palm. When his eyes flew open, she withdrew her hand.

It was a good thing the lights were turned down because he wouldn't be able to see her cheeks burning. "Um ... I wasn't sure if you were sleeping."

"I was," he said. "Deeply too. I was dreaming." Rubbing his hand down his face, he sat up and stretched his arms over his head. "It's getting late. I should go."

"Oh." She tried not to sound disappointed. "Yeah, I guess. I need to open tomorrow."

They got up from the couch, and Anders picked up the dirty plates and the half-empty boxes and brought them to the kitchen, while she straightened up the couch and living room.

"I'll see you, Darcey," he said, poking his head through the living room doorway. "Goodnight." And then he disappeared.

Her swan beat its wings inside her, urging her to follow him. For once, she agreed. Like Sarah said, things couldn't go on like this. And seeing him tonight, she knew what had been bothering her all this time.

"Wait!" she called as she flew out the door. "Anders!"

Anders was already halfway down the driveway, but upon hearing her voice, pivoted and was by her side in half a second. "What's wrong?" he said in a panicked tone. "Are you all right? Not feeling good? Is it the baby?"

"No, no." She shook her head. But how to begin? "Anders, why are you doing all this?"

"What do you mean?"

"The gifts, the food, following me around ... why?"

His face turned dark. "I thought it was obvious."

"What's obvious?"

Frowning, he shoved his hands in his pockets. "I'm trying to be a better man, Darcey."

"Better?"

"Yeah. Better for you. And our baby."

She stared at him as it all clicked in her head. "Better?" she chuckled. "Oh God."

A look of hurt crossed his face, and before he could turn away, she grabbed his hand and tugged. "Anders. Tell me what this is *really* about."

There was an uncertainty in his eyes that she couldn't miss. And a vulnerability that she didn't think she'd ever seen before. "He came to me a couple weeks ago. Christopher. My ... brother."

She gave his hand a squeeze. "Go on."

"He asked me who I was, and I wouldn't answer. Told him to ask his mother. That was the day I went to see you for lunch and you were with Cam." His mouth pulled back into a grim line.

Oh no. No wonder he'd been distraught. He sought her out and found her with another guy.

He continued. "The kid must've taken my advice, because Felicia showed up at my house days later. Threatened me if I ever told her kid about who I really was ..." Something caught in his throat. "And I lost it. God." His fists balled tight at his sides. "I was so tempted ... I went to The Den to try and drink it all away. Like what my old man would do. I haven't had a drink in over a decade, not since he died of liver failure."

"Anders—"

"But you were right. She's still living in my head ... and I let her stay there. But I don't want that anymore, Darcey. I want to be a better man. For you. For our—our baby." A sob broke from his mouth.

And that's when she finally understood him. Really understood who he was. This frustrating, infuriating, wonderful man full of contradictions. "Anders why would you go through all this trouble?"

"I told you—"

"Shh." She put a finger over his lips. "Right now, doing all of this, you're still letting them get to you. Letting your past live inside you, and making you feel like you're not good enough. But can't you see? You've gotten past all that already, even before you met me. You're the man who spends his free time teaching kids who have no one to believe in them believe in themselves. The man who won't stand for women being taken advantage of, not if he can help it. You don't need to be a better man, Anders, because *you already are*." And somehow in that revelation, she realized something too. She didn't need to be the New Darcey. The Old Darcey was just fine. All this time, she'd been strong and independent, not like Sarah was, but in her own way.

Anders stared at her, his face frozen in shock.

"And I want *that* Anders." Her heart beat like a drum in her heart as she gambled and played her last card. "When he's ready to come back, tell him to come see me." Turning around, she walked in and closed the door behind her.

Excitement, but also nervousness, filled her as she scampered to her room. Quickly, she unlocked the door and sat back on her bed. Her stomach clenched as she wondered if he would understand what she was trying to say.

Her answer was the sound of the door sliding opening. Her

chest burst with joy as Anders drew back the curtains and stalked inside her room. *There,* her swan seemed to say. *There he is. Our mate.*

"Anders." His name barely left her lips when he pounced on her, pinning her body to the bed.

"Darcey. Darcey." He repeated her name like a prayer, kissing her mouth, her cheeks, her temple. He pressed his forehead against hers. "I love you, Darcey. I want to be your mate, a dad to our child. All our kids. You have a place in my life and that's here, in my bed and by my side. I want you to be mine. Claimed and bonded." He growled against her mouth, and a primal thrill ran up her spine. "And I won't let you leave this bed until that happens. You're going to beg me to stop, but I won't. Not until I hear those three words. I'll go all night if I have to."

"That sounds ... inconvenient and awkward." Her mouth quirked up into a smile. "What will we do when Daniel or Sarah or Adam comes knocking in the morning?"

"I'll tell them they can fuck right off." He nipped at her lips. "Be mine, Darcey."

"I'm already yours." She pulled him down for a kiss. "I love you."

As he swooped down to kiss her, something strange began to happen. It was as if a rush of water washed over her, all warm and pleasant. Then her chest tightened, like a ribbon wrapping around her and pulling tight. When she opened her eyes as Anders pulled away, she knew what had happened. "Anders ..."

His mouth dropped open, then the corners pulled up into a grin. "The bond. I can feel it."

"Me too." She could feel it linking them together in a way that was impossible to describe, but she knew was just *there.*

"Darcey."

"Yes?"

"Will you forgive me?" he began. "For the things I said? For getting jealous and accusing you of all those things? For telling you that you didn't mean anything, when you were everything to me?"

There was nothing to forgive, not anymore, she wanted to tell him that. But instead, she took his hand and placed it over her heart. "What do you think? What do you feel here?"

He closed his eyes. "Love." A smile spread across his face. "Only love." He kissed her again, deeply this time, like it had been years since their lips touched, and when he released her mouth, every molecule of oxygen had left her lungs. "I'm still going to fuck you until you beg me to stop."

She barked out a laugh. "What a romantic you are."

"I'm no Prince Charming," he began. "But I'm damned well going to make sure every day of your life—of our baby's life—is a Goddamned fairy tale."

"Stop talking and kiss me, my prince," she said, before bringing his head down for another kiss.

And then there was no more talking, not for the rest of the night.

Epilogue
A FEW WEEKS LATER ...

"How are you feeling, beautiful?" Anders asked as they stepped out into the arrivals hall of Perth Airport.

"Nervous?" Not that he needed to ask, because he could sense her anxiety through their mate bond.

"Yeah." Darcey's eyes darted around. "But that's normal, right?"

"Of course." Placing his arm around her, he pressed a kiss to her temple. "But it'll be fine, I promise."

The smile she gave him warmed his heart. "I know. You're here with me."

"Always, beautiful." He kissed her again, then looked around. "I'm sure he'll be here soon."

Her hand went to her mouth. "Oh God, I think I'm gonna throw up."

"Breathe, Darcey." He rubbed his hand down her back. But who could blame her? She was about to meet her biological father for the first time.

A few weeks ago, Adam had come through on his research and found Jack Kelly. He was still alive and lived with his bevy in Perth. With Darcey's permission, Adam contacted him via email, and he responded right away. Though shocked at the discovery that his affair with Elizabeth had produced a child, Jack Kelly had been ecstatic that Darcey was alive and well, and invited her to come and visit him in Australia.

Darcey was hesitant to go, especially since Sarah and Daniel hadn't gone on a honeymoon yet and the store was still new. "Darce, if you don't go now, you won't be able to go when you pop or when the baby comes," Sarah had said. "Everything will be fine here, and Daniel and I can wait."

So, they planned the trip to go to Australia. And since they were going all the way there anyway, Anders added a side jaunt to Japan so Darcey could meet Sensei Toyama. They visited him for a few days and then drove up to Kouri Island where Anders presented her with a stunning, princess-cut diamond, which she was now wearing on her left ring finger.

"I'm glad you came with me." She smiled up at him.

"Like I would let you leave my side," he snorted and then pressed a hand to her belly protectively. The thought that he would be a father in a few months made him sweat bullets. In fact, he was still both ecstatic and horrified at the thought. Would he even make a good dad? What if he messed up? What if his kid hated him?

"Stop." A stern look crossed her face. "I know what you're thinking and feeling. You have to stop doubting yourself."

"I'm trying." For her, he tried very hard. But the doubt was always there, in the corner of his mind. How could he be a good father when his own family was messed up? When even now, he was still unsure of his future with them?

"You're thinking about the past again," Darcey said.

"I'm sorry."

"No, no." She shook her head. "Don't be sorry. We'll get

through it. No matter what happens, I'll be here. We'll be together."

Anders had already decided to move on from Felicia, but that was going to be difficult since Christopher came to him again just a couple of days ago. The kid was nineteen after all, practically an adult and figured the story out on his own. Felicia had gone into a rage when he confronted her about her previous family, but he defied his mother to come to him. Despite all that happened, Christopher didn't want to ignore Anders's existence.

Christopher had also told him he had a younger brother and sister, both lynxes. But they were only thirteen and nine, so they decided not to say anything yet, as they didn't want any blowback from Felicia. When they were old enough and could understand, Christopher said he would tell them.

"Do you see him?" Darcey's voice pitched higher than usual.

He could feel her swan flapping its wings excitedly inside of her. "I don't—" He stopped when he saw the older man walking toward them. They had video chatted with Jack Kelly a few times, so he recognized Darcey's father right away—tall and lean, silvery hair and beard and dressed in a blue shirt and khaki pants. "There."

Her shoulders tensed, and she sucked in a breath. Kelly must have spotted them because he began to rush toward them, stopping a foot away. His aquamarine eyes fixed on Darcey, as if there was nothing else around him.

"You look so much like her," he said, his voice a hoarse whisper. "Darcey."

They stood there, staring at each other until Anders nudged her forward.

"Hello, Jack. It's nice to finally meet you," she said shyly, and offered her hand.

"C'mon now, Darce, no need for that." Kelly took her hand and pulled her in for a hug. "I'm so glad you came."

"Me too." The hug lasted for another five seconds before she pulled away. "Um, you remember Anders." She pulled him forward. "My mate. And now fiancé." She held up her hand, showing him the ring.

"Glad she said yes," Kelly said with a chuckle. Anders had emailed him privately to tell him his plans. Of course, he made it clear he was not asking for his permission—he had already gone through that with the person who had raised Darcey. Sarah had made him suffer, but he supposed he deserved it.

"You knew?" Darcey said incredulously, and the two men laughed.

"Congrats, you're a lucky bloke," Kelly said as they shook hands.

"I know." He certainly felt like the luckiest "bloke" in the world.

"Darcey," Kelly began, turning to her again. His eyes misted as he continued to drink her in, a fond smile on his face. "I can't believe you're really here. I wish I had ... I want to—"

"I know." Darcey reached out and squeezed his hand. "We'll have time to say all the things we need to say."

Kelly grinned. "Well now, look at us dawdling like a couple of old biddies. Let's head out; car's right outside. It's a long drive and everyone's eager to meet you."

———

The Perth bevy actually lived just north of the city in—where else—the Swan Valley, Western Australia's oldest wine regions. The Alpha's family owned one of the largest wineries in the area, Black Feather Farm. Right now, it was spring time in the

Southern Hemisphere, and the valley burst with a verdant growth of trees, a riotous rainbow of flowers, and acres and acres of grape vines.

They arrived at Black Feather Farm to a gregarious reception from the entire bevy. Darcey had met so many relatives that she could hardly remember all their names. Aunts, uncles, cousins, second cousins—they were all a blur, plus, the sheer number of people trying to talk to her at the same time made it hard to keep track. Of course, she and Anders were presented to the Alpha and his mate, Noah and Emily Kelly. Noah looked like an older version of Jack, though he was shorter and stockier, but just as friendly as he welcomed Darcey with a big hug and Anders with a firm handshake. Finally, Jack introduced her to his kids, her half-brother and sister, Oliver and Chloe, who were sixteen and thirteen years old.

"Ready to pack up and go to back to America yet?" Jack joked as he steered her away from the exuberant crowd and handed her a sparkling water. He knew about the pregnancy, of course, as she had told him in the car on the way here. Her heart warmed when she had seen the tears in his eyes as he struggled not to cry.

"Not yet." In truth, both she and her swan loved being around so many people like them. "Thanks." She accepted the drink and let him lead her to the back porch that looked out onto the valley. "This is stunning."

"I'm glad you think so," he said quietly. "This is your legacy, too, you know."

A comfortable silence settled over them as they continued to admire the views. Jack cleared his throat. "I really had no idea about you, Darcey. I'm so sorry. For letting you down. And letting your mother down."

"No, there's nothing to be sorry about." She had told him

about Elizabeth over the video call, and he had been shocked and saddened by the news. She also relayed what had happened with Cassius, and how he'd been stripped of his Alpha status and was now in jail, awaiting trial for Darcey's kidnapping and attempted murder. Jack had wanted to fly over right away and get revenge for her and her mother, but she convinced him to stay put.

"If I had known, I would have come for you," he said. "You could have grown up here. With us. With me."

"But I didn't," she said. "And, well ... I'm kind of glad." Her gaze turned to Anders, who was already surrounded by her various aunts, uncles, and cousins as he told some funny story that made them laugh.

"So, your mate is a tiger, huh?" he teased.

"I didn't believe it either," she said. "Did you know right away? About my mother?"

"Know what?"

"That she was your mate. I felt like my whole life, I was looking for something. Did you feel that way? And what about when you met?"

Jack's face turned serious. "I'm sorry, Darcey. But Elizabeth wasn't my mate."

"She wasn't? But Cassius said you guys were."

"I'm not sure where he got that idea." He scratched his head. "When I met Elizabeth, I have to admit I was infatuated. She was so gorgeous, just like you. I resisted her, of course, but then she confessed to me that she and Cassius weren't really mates, and she was unhappy. I know it's not an excuse, but I did fall for her. I told her that if she wanted to get away, I'd help her get out of that situation. But then Noah and I had to come back home, and I never heard from her again. I thought that maybe she decided to continue on with the lie. It was none of my business, after all. But I would never have guessed that she would get pregnant. Anyway, years later, I met Janice—that's Oliver and Chloe's mum—who's my mate. She died a couple of years ago."

The profound grief in his eyes was unmistakable.

"You survived her death."

"Had to." He nodded at his kids. "For them."

She frowned. "I don't understand though. My mom died of a broken heart. Cassius pretty much confirmed it. So, if you weren't mates, why did she die?"

"Isn't it obvious, Darcey?" He cupped her chin and caressed her cheeks. "She had to give up the one person she loved the most."

Tears burned at her eyes. She'd always told herself that her mother had loved her, but now she knew that was the truth.

"It's all right, love." Jack brushed the tears away from her face. "You're home now."

"Darcey, a little help!"

"Anders?" She turned her head toward the sound of his voice. "What's going on?"

Her mate strode over to them, looking sheepish. "Your relatives are pretty ... uh ... lively." He shot Jack an apologetic look.

The older man laughed. "They can be a rowdy bunch. Oi!" He called. "Stop annoying my future son-in-law, ya buggers! And where's the tucker? We're starving. Do I have to do everything myself?" He shook his head. "Darcey love, Anders, will you excuse me? I should check on the food." With a last parting grin, he walked away.

"You okay?" she asked Anders.

"Yeah ... just overwhelmed." He frowned then lowered his voice. "Their accents—I can't understand what they're saying, so I just keep nodding along. And then they started asking me questions. I promised your Uncle Angus that I'd let him take me to the outback, or give him one of my kidneys, I'm not sure."

She giggled. "I'm sure it'll be fine. You can live with one kidney."

"Oh, *ha ha*." He placed an arm around her and gazed out into the valley. "It sure is nice out here."

With a sigh, she leaned into him. "It is."

"You must be happy, now that you're home."

The comment made her nose wrinkle. Jack had said the same thing. But her swan didn't agree, and neither did she.

"Home? Oh no. Don't get me wrong, I'm happy knowing I'm not the only one of my kind, and I like being around them. But I don't belong here; this isn't my home." Taking his hands in hers, she wrapped his arms around her and laid her head against his chest. "This." The beating of his heart filled her ears like the most beautiful rhythm in the world. "*This* is my home."

And for the first time in her life, she was truly done searching.

————

If you want to read a hot, sexy bonus scene from this book just join my newsletter here

http://aliciamontgomeryauthor.com/mailing-list/

You'll get access to ALL the bonus materials from all my books and my **FREE** novella **The Last Blackstone Dragon.**

But we're not done yet.
Krieger's secret is out.
What's he been doing all these months?

And how is that connected to a certain redhead fashion designer?

Find out by reading the next book

Blackstone Ranger Guardian

Available at selected online bookstores.

Turn the page for a special preview.

A FEW MONTHS AGO ...

The humungous grizzly bear trudged through the blanket of snow on the ground, unbothered by neither the dangerously low temperatures nor the fast falling flakes piling up on its large block head and burly body. It continued to lumber along the through the trees, going farther up the mountain.

Up here, John Krieger allowed his animal to take over their shared body. With the bear in charge, their senses remained sharp, their body could hold up agains the elements, while the human side remained dull and suppressed.

It was the only place safe enough to allow the beast its freedom.

A howl in the distance made the bear pause. Krieger recognized the sound, as did his bear. *Milos*. He was their nearest their neighbor—if he could be called that. He had never seen the wolf shifter in human skin, but Damon had told him about the other man's presence on the mountain when he arrived about a year ago. Since then, the two of them had encountered each other a handful of times, both in animal form. While many in the past would have turned tail and run, the one-eyed wolf showed no fear in the presence of the mighty grizzly. In fact, Kreiger had not sensed much of anything at all in the other shifter, except maybe recognizing their sameness. Here was another broken animal, hiding out from the world.

A few heartbeats passed and there was no more howling. Was it a warning? Of what? Up here, near the highest peaks of the Blackstone Mountains, there were no dangers, at least not to apex predators like them. There was hardly anything or anyone up here at all, not in the dead of winter. The real bears were all deep in their den, hibernating. Perhaps there might be an odd shifter or two, but that was rare in this weather.

The grizzly continued on. They had a job to do, after all, and Krieger took his work as a Blackstone ranger seriously, guarding the entrance to Contessa Peak for the last five years. There were a few hikers who dared scale the peak in better weather, so he always made sure they made it up and back down safely.

Mostly, though, it was shifters who roamed up here. After all, this was a sanctuary for all of their kind who lived in Blackstone, the one place they could truly feel safe in their animal skins. It was his job too, to protect them and make sure they remained undisturbed.

Of course, there were the shifters that didn't need protection, that is, they were the ones who protected the entirety of Blackstone itself. The Lennoxes were a family of dragons—four in total—who owned the mountains and the minerals in them that had made them one of the richest families in the world. Though Krieger had never met any of them personally, he'd seen them several times in the last few years, flying and dipping like gigantic graceful butterflies as they chased each other or conducted flying races, using the jagged crown of Contessa Peak as a finish line. The largest one was the sire, and then there were two twin males who were indistinguishable from each other, and the smaller female one, who seemed just as fierce as her brothers.

Yes, he took this job seriously. It was not only his life, but also his salvation, allowing him to live out and remain undisturbed for the most part. Encounters with others were far and few between, he made sure of that. He used his excellent sense of hearing and smell to keep track of who and what was up and around Contessa Peak. If he found a lost hiker or shifter, it was easy enough to call HQ to have them picked up or rescued, watching over them until help came. Rarely did he come near others. No, it was too much. Too risky.

He continued on, rounding the perimeter of his patrol area. All rangers on duty had a schedule and a route to follow, but his sole area was responsibility remained the same. It didn't matter what day it was or what time is was. There was a sheet of paper tacked up in his cabin with his hours and days of duty, but it had been so faded he could barely read the print. For him, there were no weekends, no vacations, no off hours. Contessa Peak was his responsibility, his to protect at all hours, all days. The patrol, the job, the guard, that was all that mattered to him and his bear. They were entrusted by the Chief and the Blackstone Dragons to keep everyone here safe, and so that's what they would do. He was very good at following orders, after all.

The wind, which had already been whipping when he left his little cabin, had now picked up. As the minutes and hours passed, it grew stronger, blowing sleet across the mountains. *Not good*, Krieger thought. A freak snowstorm, perhaps.

The CB radio he had in his cabin was the only form of communication he had to the outside world. He relied on it for information, from which ranger worked what area to alerts for lost hikers, but more important, weather for the day. The dispatcher hadn't said anything about a storm coming this morning so it must have blown in from out of nowhere.

Need to turn back, he told his bear. Sure, if things got rough, they could probably dig a den in the ground and hold up until it passed, but why bother when he knew exactly where they were and how far the walk back to the cabin was? Despite the nearly white-out conditions, his keen sense of direction was like a compass, keeping him oriented at all times.

The bear lumbered around, but halted halfway. *What the hell—*

There.

His grizzly picked up on it before he did. The sound was faint, but it was there.

Small, slowing faint footsteps of four paws trudging through snow.

A pathetic scritch-scratch sound.

A heartbeat.

Someone was out there. And they were in trouble.

Bear and man were one in body and mind as they focused their senses. Nearby, for sure. The bear followed the sounds, like a beacon in the white vastness of the storm. The footsteps had stopped now. Then the little panting sounds. Until finally it was just the patter of the heartbeat, slowing down to a near halt.

Six feet to the left, about two feet below the snow.

How he and his bear knew where the sounds came from, Krieger didn't question. There was only the need to find out whatever it was and help them. The layer of snow was no match for the bear's paws as it dug through the ice like it was paper. Finally, buried underneath all that white, bits of red fur began to appear. Krieger had to slow his animal down, directing its sharp claws to dig around the poor, half-frozen creature, and pull it out.

Huh.

It was so small in his giant paws, but it was obvious now what it was, from the reddish and gray fur, pointed snout and ears, plus the black-tipped paws. A fox. It's bushy red tail hung down, limp like the rest of its body.

Poor thing. Its ragged breaths and faintly beating heart told him the creature was still alive but just barely. *Shifter*, his animal instinct whispered.

His bear roared loudly, a garbled sound his ears couldn't decipher. It was as if it was trying to catch his attention, telling him something.

Need to get out of the cold. Get it warm and dry, in the cabin. He usually avoided direct contact with hikers and other shifters, but there was no time to contact HQ nor would he leave this creature out in the cold to freeze to death. Carefully tucking it into the crook of its arm, the bear got two feet and began the long walk back to their den.

The fox didn't stir or make any more sounds in their arms. *Out cold*. Shifters were stronger than their human or animal counterparts, but they still had their limits. Maybe this little creature overestimated theirs or it too had been caught in the sudden storm. He could imagine that it got lost, then turned around then the storm came in.

Finally, he spied the light of his cabin in the distance. By now the storm was in full force, and if he didn't have his sense of direction or keen senses, he would have been lost too. His strength though, had dwindled down from all that work, so he shifted back to his human form as he trudged up the porch steps, now fully human as his hand reached for the door knob and staggered inside.

The lights flickered overhead before dying, plunging the cabin into darkness. *Got here just in time, thank fuck*.

He was bone tired, but he still had his little friend to think about. The fox remained tucked into the crook of his now-human arm. It looked bigger than he initially thought, a full grown adult, he reckoned. Still, it didn't move. The breathing was more even now, but its body remained heavy, perhaps conserving its energy to heal itself. He could relate—he too was bone tired. So, he stumbled toward the largest piece of furniture in the single living space in his cabin—the bed—and collapsed on top of it. As his eye lids grew heavier and heavier, he tucked the fox closer to his body, sharing his warmth, then passed out cold, but not before he swore he could make out what his bear was trying to say.

Mine.

Printed in the USA
CPSIA information can be obtained
at www.ICGtesting.com
LVHW100400130823
754932LV00002B/341